BETRAYAL OF TRUST

ADVANCE PRAISE FOR BETRAYAL OF TRUST

"Tense, intelligent, and relentlessly engaging, *Betrayal of Trust* is a standout in the genre. From its explosive opening to the final twist, the novel delivers a sophisticated blend of scientific intrigue and psychological drama. Cooper's writing is crisp and confident, bringing complex characters and high-stakes research to vivid life. A must-read for anyone who appreciates thrillers with brains and bite." —Kyle Eaton, *Seattle Book Review*

"Cooper probes the dark undercurrents of academic medicine, where reputation shields predation and victims are too easily dismissed. For readers who like their science sharp and their stakes personal, this one cuts deep." —*The Prairies Book Review*

"A gripping medical thriller that delivers both emotional depth and razor-sharp suspense. *Betrayal of Trust* masterfully explores themes of ambition, revenge, and the consequences of unchecked power in the world of cancer research. The dynamic between Brad and Karen is compelling, but it's the story's raw portrayal of justice that makes this installment unforgettable. Geoffrey M. Cooper has crafted a tale that is both timely and unflinchingly bold." —Kathryn Dare, *San Diego Book Review*

PRAISE FOR EARLIER BRAD PARKER AND KAREN RICHMOND MEDICAL THRILLERS

Nondisclosure

"One of this year's best mysteries by a Maine writer . . . a gritty mystery, well-crafted with a complex, intriguing plot, tense suspense, vivid action and wholly believable characters." —Bill Bushnell, *Central Maine Sentinel*

Forever

"A medical thriller on the lines of a Robin Cook–style saga . . . designed to keep readers on edge to its satisfying conclusion." —D. Donovan, *Midwest Book Review*

"A persuasive tale of scientific intrigue." —*Kirkus Reviews*

Bad Medicine

"Plot twists and fast-paced action make this a fun yet scary story." —Bill Bushnell, *Central Maine Sentinel*

"A noteworthy whodunit with unexpected plot twists." — *Kirkus Reviews*

Ill Intent

"A whodunit that effortlessly navigates a complex plot and deepens its narrator's characterization." —*Kirkus Reviews*

"A medical thriller that is firmly rooted in psychological interactions and unexpected developments." —D. Donovan, *Midwest Book Review*

Perilous Obsession

"*Perilous Obsession* is Ogunquit author Geoffrey Cooper's fifth mystery in his thriller series featuring Brad Parker and FBI Special

Agent Karen Richmond. And this is probably the best one of all."
—Bill Bushnell, *Central Maine Sentinel*

"An often-exciting tale of medical malfeasance and wide-ranging criminality." —*Kirkus Reviews*

The Fifth Student

"College students cheating on a test sizzles into something far more complex and deadly in the latest thriller from Geoffrey Cooper." —Matt Cost, award-winning author of *Velma Gone Awry* and the Clay Wolfe/Port Essex and Mainely Mystery series.

"A zippy, tricky academic murder mystery." —*Kirkus Reviews*

The Third Man

"Falling between Robin Cook's medical thrillers and Robert Parker's Spenser potboilers isn't a bad place to live—and this one hits a sweet spot." —*Blue Ink Review*

The Plagiarism Plot

"Brad Parker and his crime-fighting fiancée Karen Richmond unravel a case of plagiarism that leaves dead bodies in its wake. Cooper's jaundiced take on academia's rarefied air combined with Parker's scientific approach and Karen's no-nonsense pragmatism make for an engaging police procedural that uncovers the malice underlying academia's poised facade." —*BlueInk Review*

BETRAYAL OF TRUST

A MEDICAL THRILLER

BRAD PARKER AND KAREN RICHMOND
BOOK 9

GEOFFREY M COOPER

CAPTAIN THOMAS PUBLISHING

To two special friends who were undergoing cancer treatment while this book was being written.

Ulla Hansen (1953-2025), my closest friend and colleague for forty years.

And Deborah Dobie (1952-2025), Audrey's best friend since college.

BETRAYAL OF TRUST

CHAPTER 1
SHIRLEY

She got to the auditorium early and grabbed a seat in the third row. An audience of close to a thousand was expected, and she wanted to be close enough to have a good view of the bastard's face as he presented his lecture. A lecture she vowed to make his last.

Anger consumed her as she watched Eric Salton, nattily dressed in a black dinner jacket, accept the award for Outstanding Achievement in Clinical Cancer Research. Then he strode arrogantly to the podium and began talking about his work on melistomab, which he immodestly claimed was the most effective treatment for lung cancer to have been developed in years. He began by discussing the laboratory results and then reviewed the initial clinical trial, in which his team had first documented the striking activity of melistomab against advanced lung cancers. Based on that early success, they'd moved on to a large trial with nearly a thousand patients, and those results proved unequivocally that melistomab was far better than any other available treatment. Followed, of course, by FDA approval, so melistomab was now available to everyone.

Shirley's blood boiled as she listened to the audience applaud.

She knew what he was really like. A piece of shit who never thought of anyone besides himself, devoid of any feelings of empathy. People who trusted him were just objects to be used and discarded at his convenience. No better than laboratory rats.

A small crowd surrounded Salton when he stepped down from the podium, and she watched as he shook hands and chatted with admirers until the group dispersed. Then he left the auditorium with a man about Salton's age and a young woman who looked like she was in her late twenties. Probably one of Salton's students, twenty-five or thirty years younger than he was.

She'd hoped to catch him alone after his lecture, but she shrugged off her disappointment and followed at a safe distance as they walked through the passageway from the Hynes Convention Center to the Sheraton Boston Hotel and went into the lobby lounge. Probably for celebratory drinks, she thought, as she took a seat in one of the plush leather chairs toward the side of the lobby, where she could keep her eyes on the lounge entrance. Maybe she'd be able to get to him when he came out.

Twenty minutes later, the other man left by himself, leaving Salton alone with the young woman. Shirley figured he was probably getting ready to hit on her. That would be his style. If he was successful, her own plans for tonight would be spoiled.

But luck was on her side. It was no more than another five minutes before the young woman came out of the lounge alone, glanced nervously over her shoulder, and hurried across the lobby to the elevator bank. Maybe Salton *had* tried to hit on her, and she'd shot him down. It didn't matter. Whatever had happened, he was alone now.

She only had to wait a few more minutes before Salton left the lounge by himself. Her time had come.

She got up and hurried across the lobby to catch up to him. "Dr. Salton," she called out, "I'm so excited to run into you!" She gave him the eager smile that usually worked. Especially with older men. "I heard your lecture; it was fabulous, and I'd love to talk to you. I apologize for waylaying you like this; I know how busy you must be, but I'd be really grateful if you could spare me just a few minutes sometime."

He ran his eyes over her and returned her smile. "Not a problem, I'm pleased to meet you. But you have me at a disadvantage." He extended his hand. "I'm Eric."

"And I'm Shirley. Shirley Leavitt." She took his hand and held it for longer than necessary. "Thank you so much. I'm a student from NYU, and the group I work with has some results from a drug trial that I'd really like to show you. We're not quite sure where to go from here, and it'd be just great to get your thoughts on it."

"Sure, I'd be happy to take a look." He gestured toward the lounge. "Why don't we talk over a drink?"

She could tell she had him. Even easier than she'd hoped. "I'd love to, but I don't have a printout of the data to show you."

"That's okay. We can look at it on your iPad or whatever you have with you."

She sighed. "I'm afraid all I have is a thumb drive." Then she gave him her most seductive smile. "Do you have a computer we could use?"

"No problem. I brought my laptop to the meeting with me. I'm staying right here in the hotel, so it'll just take me a few minutes to run up to my room and get it. Do you want to go ahead and get a table in the lounge for us?"

"Oh, why don't I go upstairs with you instead?" She moved close to him and squeezed his arm. "Maybe we can have a drink in your room and look at my data there. I'm sure that'd be more comfortable."

His face lit up with anticipation. *Gotcha*, she thought.

He took her arm and guided her toward the elevator. She pressed against him as they rode up to his floor and went down the hall to his room. When he opened the door, she moved in for a kiss.

When they were finally in his room and had come up for air, she asked if she could use the bathroom to get ready. He'd taken off his dinner jacket and was starting to turn down the bed when she came out. Naked.

"I'm ready now, Eric," she purred.

He turned to her, and she watched his crotch start to bulge at the sight of her nude body. Then he noticed the knife in her hand, and she smiled as she saw his lust turn to fear.

He started to say something, maybe to protest or beg. But she sunk her blade deep into his chest before he had a chance.

Now that the job was done, she let her rage loose and plunged her knife into him again. And then again, and again. His chest, his stomach, his face . . . everywhere her blade could find a home until her fury was finally spent.

Then she took a shower to wash his blood off, got dressed, and took a final look at his mutilated corpse. She recalled that someone had said, "Revenge is a dish best served cold." But she decided it was better enjoyed hot.

Composed again, she locked the door behind her, took the elevator down to the lobby, and walked several blocks east to where she'd parked her car. When she was halfway through the drive home, she stopped at a gas station and used the restroom to wash off her makeup, remove the contacts, and discard the wig.

But she kept the knife. There was more work to be done.

CHAPTER 2

BRAD

Karen was still in bed when I finished dressing to go downstairs and meet Eric Salton for breakfast. She'd driven down from our house in Maine yesterday afternoon so we could spend a couple of days together in Boston at the tail-end of the cancer research conference. After spending the last four days alone, I'd been delighted to see her. Thrilled, in fact. A hotel room was a whole lot nicer with Karen in it.

Last night we'd taken advantage of the pleasant spring weather, a welcome change from the steady rain that had fallen for most of April, to take a walk through my old neighborhood of Back Bay. From our hotel on Boylston Street, we'd gone up to Newbury, window-shopped for a bit, and then crossed over to Comm Ave. The cherry trees on Commonwealth Mall were in full bloom, so we enjoyed a colorful stroll past my old condo to the Public Garden. From there we walked around the pond, stopping to admire the Swan Boats, and had dinner at a French bistro on Boylston before returning to our hotel. Where we did our level best to make up for the last several nights of separation.

My plan for today was to attend just one talk after having

breakfast with Eric. Then I was going to play hooky for the rest of the day so Karen and I could enjoy a leisurely visit to the Museum of Fine Arts, a classic Boston haunt that had always been one of our favorites when we lived here.

But just as I was bending down to kiss her before I left, someone knocked on the door to our room. Karen jumped up and threw on one of the hotel's terrycloth robes, while I went to the door and asked who was there.

Whoever it was simply said, "Police" and held a badge up to the peephole. I opened the door and was surprised to see Stan Zelen, a Boston homicide detective Karen had known from back when she'd been an FBI agent in the Boston office. I'd met Zelen last year when my friend and colleague Carolyn Gelman had been wrongfully accused of murder. Despite the uncomfortable circumstances, he and I somehow hit it off and developed a liking for each other.

"Zelen!" I exclaimed. "Didn't expect you to show up here."

He grinned. "Hope it's not too much of a shock, Parker. How you doing? And how's your better half?"

"No shock, it's nice to see you again. I'm fine, and Karen can speak for herself."

Zelen's smile broadened as he spotted Karen in her bathrobe. "You're a surprise; I wasn't expecting to see you today. And judging from your outfit, I'd guess you weren't expecting me either. Or do you always dress so formally for visitors?"

"Oh, shut up, Zelen," Karen laughed. "Any more crap like that and I'll bring harassment charges against you. But what's up? Or did you just drop by to see Brad because the two of you became bros last year?"

Zelen's expression turned serious. "I'm afraid I do have some business. Brad, do you know Eric Salton?"

A question like that from a homicide detective didn't bode well, and I had a bad feeling as I answered. "I'm actually supposed to meet him for breakfast this morning. Why?"

"I know, I saw your meeting in his calendar," Zelen replied. "I'm sorry to tell you, he was murdered last night."

"Christ! What happened? A robbery?"

He shook his head. "No, it wasn't a robbery. He was knifed in his room, just two floors above you. Nothing was taken, including a wallet stuffed full of cash and a fancy watch. Did you know him well?"

"Not really," I said. "We were professional acquaintances, not personal friends."

"So the meeting you had planned with him this morning was to talk shop?"

"Yeah. Eric is—was—an expert in running clinical trials of new cancer drugs. We have a couple of candidates coming along at MTRI, and I wanted to see if he'd be interested in working with us."

Zelen took out a notebook. "Let me just make sure I have this straight. MTRI is the Maine Translational Research Institute in Wells, right? And you're still the director?"

"Right," I confirmed. "Is that relevant? If it wasn't a robbery, what do you think happened?"

"We don't have much to go on at this point, so we're trying to put together as much background on the victim as we can. The killer kept going at him after he was dead, stabbed him at least a dozen times all over his face and body. So it was pretty clearly angry and personal. Do you know anything about his private life?"

"Nothing to speak of. I know he was married. And I've heard that he had a reputation for being a bit of a player with young women, possibly including some of his students."

"We heard that too," Zelen said. "Maybe he had something going on last night that went wrong. Badly."

"How about his wife?" Karen chimed in. "It sounds like the kind of rage you might see from a spouse who's been cheated on."

Zelen nodded. "Yeah, the wife was my first thought, too. But it doesn't look like she's it. Two of our guys saw her earlier this morning to do the notification. They say she has a solid alibi for last night. Anyway, the killer left plenty of DNA in Salton's room. It's not a match to anything in the database, but we can use it to follow up any suspects, including the wife. I'm pretty sure it'll rule her out."

"If it's not the wife, I'd put someone he had a fling with next in the line of suspects," Karen suggested. "Or a student he harassed. But if he was killed in his room, don't you have video to go with your DNA evidence? The hotel's bound to be chock full of security cameras."

"Sure, we've got plenty of video. Between that and talking to a couple of his colleagues, we can pretty well piece together what happened. Just not who did it or why."

He took out his phone and showed us a picture. "This is almost certainly the killer, who incidentally looks at least twenty years younger than Salton's wife. Brad, any chance you recognize her? Maybe she's attending the meeting."

The picture was a close-up of a young woman, probably in her twenties, with long red hair and green eyes. I tried, but had to tell Zelen that I didn't think I'd seen her before.

"Why do you think she's your perp?" Karen asked. "It looks like this was taken in the hotel lobby."

"It was," Zelen confirmed. "Right before she picked the victim up. We have video of everything that happened after he came back to the hotel last night following some award lecture he gave in the convention center."

"I was in the audience," I noted. "The award's a big deal, given annually by the American Association for Cancer Research at this meeting. His lecture was at four in the afternoon."

"Did you talk to him afterward?"

"I tried, but he was surrounded by a crowd of rabid fans, so I settled for just giving him a congratulatory thumbs-up."

Zelen nodded and consulted his notebook. "I talked to two of his colleagues, Travis Lane and Stephanie Morris, who waited it out and then came back here with Salton for a drink. Video shows the three of them entering the hotel a little after five thirty. They were followed at a safe distance by our suspect, who waited in the lobby while they went into the lounge."

"You think she followed them back and waited with the intention of killing Salton?" I asked.

"Exactly. According to Travis Lane, Salton's plan for the evening was to hit on Stephanie. He wanted Lane to join the two of them for a drink, so that she'd feel comfortable going to the lounge. But then Lane was supposed to leave the two of them alone, which he did. After Lane left, Stephanie says that Salton tried to proposition her, but she turned him down. Then she left him alone in the lounge, and the video shows him leaving the lounge about five minutes after she did."

"And your suspect was waiting in the lobby?" Karen asked.

"Right. As soon as Salton came back into the lobby, she hopped up and approached him. I've got that part of the video on my phone, let me show you their interaction."

We watched the woman get up from her seat and hurry across the lobby to Salton. They talked for a few minutes, and then he took her arm and guided her to the elevator. The video followed them in the elevator, where they stood close together, and then down the hall to his room, where they kissed passionately before going in.

Zelen put the phone back in his pocket. "That was six thirty-three. The next we see is her leaving the room twenty minutes later. Nobody else goes in or out for the rest of the night, and the ME puts the time of death between six and seven."

"Certainly looks like she's your perp," Karen agreed. "But I'd expect her to have been covered in blood after a frenzied knife murder. How'd she get out of the hotel without someone raising an alarm?"

Zelen snorted. "No blood. She was just as clean when she left his room as she was while sitting in the lobby. It looks like she showered after killing him and must have taken her clothes off to do the job. That's where we got her DNA; lots left in the bathroom."

"Sounds well-planned," Karen commented. "Did she bring the knife with her?"

"We think so. There wasn't anything in the room, and the ME says it was a six- or seven-inch serrated blade. Probably a hunting knife."

"Do you think the killer's a pro?" I wondered. "Maybe the wife hired someone."

Karen shook her head. "No, a pro wouldn't have left DNA evidence behind. This has to be somebody who knows they don't already have DNA in a database that can be matched to samples from the crime scene."

"How about facial recognition?" I asked. "Couldn't she be identified by searching something like driver's license photos?"

"Possibly, but everybody knows hotels use security cameras, and it wouldn't have been hard for her to disguise herself," Karen pointed out. "A wig, colored contact lenses, and makeup is all it would take."

Zelen grunted. "I'm afraid you might be right. In which case, we'll need to identify suspects and hope for a DNA match. I'll start with the wife and Stephanie to be sure and then work on ferreting out a list of our victim's past romantic involvements."

"I'd focus on young women like Stephanie who worked with him and might have been harassed or threatened," Karen suggested. "That can create a lot of anger."

Zelen gave her a mock salute. "Good idea, chief. Guess that's why they made you the boss of one of Maine's major crimes units. But worry not, I've already subpoenaed his employment records to check for complaints."

CHAPTER 3

I squirmed in my seat, unable to concentrate on the one talk I'd wanted to go to this morning. It wasn't the speaker's fault. She was giving a good, clear presentation of interesting data. But I couldn't get my mind off Eric Salton's murder.

When she finally finished, I went back upstairs to get Karen, and we took off for the MFA. Karen had gotten tickets for a Georgia O'Keeffe exhibit, and I'd been looking forward to it. Not only because Karen and I were going to spend the afternoon together— which was reason enough—but also because I was interested in seeing the paintings O'Keeffe had done at York Beach. Although people didn't particularly think of her as a Maine artist, she'd vacationed on Long Sands Beach, about twenty miles south of our house on Drakes Island, from 1920 to 1928, and several paintings from that period were included in the exhibit. Two of them, *Wave, Night* and *Sun Water Maine*, made it easy for me to imagine that I was walking on our beach at home with my pug, Rosie.

Despite my anticipation, the O'Keeffe exhibit failed to purge Salton from my thoughts. I was just too distracted to enjoy it. Which was something Karen didn't miss.

As soon as we left the exhibit, she asked what I'd thought of O'Keeffe's sculptures. I couldn't remember what we'd seen, but I knew that O'Keeffe had done some sculptures in addition to her paintings, so I faked a response. "They were great. Like all her work."

That got me Karen's raised eyebrow look. "Uh-huh. Except there wasn't any sculpture in this exhibit."

I managed an embarrassed laugh. "I'm sorry, I thought I must have skipped over them because I wasn't paying attention. My mind's elsewhere."

"I noticed. Eric Salton's taken it over, I assume?"

"I'm afraid so. I can't stop thinking of him. He might have been guilty of harassment, but he didn't deserve what happened."

Karen led us over to a bench, and we sat down. "I agree. Maybe he should have been fired, but nobody deserves to die like that."

"Do you think that's what happened? That he was killed by one of his victims?"

"If Zelen's right that it wasn't the wife, I think that's the most likely scenario. But we're getting a bit ahead of ourselves. As far as I can tell, we don't really know what kind of sexual misconduct he was guilty of. If he intimidated or threatened women into having sex with him, it's not hard to imagine one of them taking a bloody revenge. But if he slept with willing partners, I'm not so sure. Have you heard anything about the nature of his activities?"

I shook my head. "Only what I told Zelen earlier. He had a reputation for playing around, and there were rumors that his partners included young women who worked for him. I don't even know how much of that's true, let alone whether his partners were coerced. Do you think Zelen will be able to get to the bottom of it?"

She shrugged. "He's a good cop, and checking Salton's personnel file is a smart first move. Anyone angry enough to kill him may have tried filing a complaint. And talking to present and former members of his group should eventually sort out whether the rumors are true, as well as getting Zelen started on developing a list of Salton's partners. Or victims."

"Presumably one of them will be recognizable from the killer's photo. Or could she have been too well disguised to identify that way?" I asked.

She waved a hand dismissively. "Doesn't matter. You can't disguise DNA."

"Can Zelen get samples from potential suspects to compare to the crime scene? Doesn't he need enough evidence to get a warrant first?"

She shook her head. "He can ask suspects to volunteer a sample, saying it's to rule them out. Very few innocent people refuse that kind of request, so anyone who does becomes a serious target of investigation. If that happened, Zelen would look further into her relationship with Salton and check out her alibi for the night of the murder. If it all fell together, he'd be able to get a warrant for her DNA."

"You make it sound easy, as long as the killer's a woman Salton harassed."

"I think that's a pretty good bet. His murder was clearly a crime of passion, which screams anger and revenge. I'm sure Zelen will look at other angles to be thorough, like money and drugs, but that's not what this case feels like. Do you have any other ideas?"

"No, women were his only vice that I know of. Other than that, he was a cancer doc who saved lives. Often the lives of patients who thought their cases were hopeless. To them, he was probably a hero."

She nodded. "All of which says that Zelen's on the right track. Since you're obviously curious, I'll keep in touch with him and see how it goes. Does Salton's death have any direct effect on you? Did you have something in the works with him?"

"Not yet, although I was hoping to get a collaboration started with him this morning. We have two promising new drugs that are ready for clinical trial, and I wanted to see if he'd be interested in working with us. We can do it ourselves at MTRI, but we have several trials running already, and our clinic is just about at capacity. I'll talk to our clinical director about it tomorrow, but I may need to figure out someone else to approach as an outside collaborator."

"Good luck, that sounds as if it might be a hassle." She glanced at her watch. "It's after two. Do you want to see some more of the museum? Or are you ready to head home?"

"Home. I probably wouldn't be able to pay attention to another exhibit anyway. A walk on the beach with Rosie sounds better."

CHAPTER 4

The disadvantage of Karen and my having come to Boston separately was that we now had two cars to drive home. I said that I'd follow her for the hour-and-a-half trip, but we both knew that wasn't going to work. I couldn't keep up with her on an open road, let alone in Boston traffic, and I lost sight of her red Volvo a few minutes after we left the hotel. I always wondered whether she used her siren when she got ahead of me like that, but she swore she didn't, claiming it was just because I drove like an old man.

When I finally got to our house on Drakes Island, Rosie came dashing to the door, so excited that she couldn't keep still long enough for me to pick her up for our usual cuddle. It took several minutes before she stopped jumping and twirling around, and she didn't really calm down until I managed to hang on to her long enough to take her over to the couch and sit down next to Karen. Only then did she finally relax and stretch out to lie across both our laps, content that her pack had reunited.

Karen laughed and bent over to give me a kiss. "I got the same high-energy greeting when I first got home. It took several minutes for her to quiet down, and then she kept watching the door for you. Maybe now that you're here, she'll get back to normal again."

I glanced at Rosie, who looked like she was ready to resume her antics. "Maybe. But why don't we take her out for a walk on the beach and let her burn off some of that excess energy? It's nice out and it's just after five thirty, so we have plenty of daylight left."

"Good idea. And we can take drinks down with us," Karen suggested. "I took out some of the frozen lasagna, so we're all set to heat that up for dinner later. And I had an interesting talk with Zelen a little while ago that I'll tell you about."

We stopped in the kitchen to get a tumbler of my favorite single malt scotch—Oban—and a glass of sauvignon blanc for Karen. Then we went out through the glass slider leading from our kitchen to the deck and down the half-dozen steps to the beach.

Being right on the ocean was one of the nicest things about our house in Maine, and a walk seemed agreeable to Rosie too. As soon as we reached the beach, she raced to the water and began her game of running into the ocean after receding waves and then back to shore when the waves rolled back in. Back and forth, back and forth, only interrupting herself occasionally to chase a seagull who'd inadvertently wandered too close.

We sipped our drinks and amused ourselves by watching her antics for several minutes. Then I asked Karen about her talk with Zelen.

"I called to tell him that you and I had kicked around possible motives a bit more and hadn't come up with anything new," she began. "Also to let him know we were curious about the case and would appreciate it if he could keep us informed. He said he'd be happy to and added that there'd already been an interesting development."

"So soon?" I was surprised. "It seemed like it'd take him quite a while to work through a list of potential suspects."

"He said he had a feeling that Stephanie hadn't told him every-thing, so he went back to talk to her again. She confirmed that

Salton made a practice of hitting on women who worked for him and had no hesitation in using his power over them. She'd been afraid that's what he intended when he first asked her to come to his award lecture, and she was sure it was coming when Salton's friend left them alone in the lounge the night he was killed. She said that Salton wasn't even subtle about it. He started off by telling her how good he thought she was and how he could help move her career forward. Then he put his hand on her thigh and suggested they go someplace more private to talk about how he could help her."

I saw red. "Damn scumbag! From my dealings with him, I'd never have guessed he'd be that much of a shit."

"Wait, it gets worse. Stephanie had been thinking about what to do if—or when—she was faced with that situation. She knew a former clinical fellow who'd turned him down, and he'd tanked her career in response. Didn't let her get involved in interesting projects, gave her mediocre evaluations, and ultimately wrote a damning letter of recommendation that killed her job prospects."

"Jesus. And Stephanie didn't want that to happen to her. Naturally enough."

"For sure. But having had time to think about it, she came up with a strategic response. Brilliant actually. She told him she loved working with him and was deeply grateful for everything he did for her. But she was sorry, she played for the other team."

"What?!" I laughed. "She got out of it by telling him she was gay?"

Karen's eyes twinkled. "Yep. She said he was so surprised that it left him speechless, and she was able to leave before he had a chance to protest. Laughing to herself."

"Smart lady," I said. Then another possibility occurred to me. "But is it possible that what she told Zelen was a cover story? What if Salton made the pass at her and she told him off, instead of having a good excuse ready. Then she got scared, threw on a quick disguise, and went back to kill him."

Karen gave me a half smile. "Not bad, we'll make a detective out of you yet. Zelen said he thought of the same thing, except the killer was on video in the lobby while Stephanie was in the lounge with Salton. He got a DNA sample from her anyway, which confirms she didn't do it."

I smacked my forehead. "Whoops, I forgot about the video of the killer in the lobby all that time. Guess I'm not ready for a gold shield just yet. But in that case, how about the other woman Stephanie told Zelen about? The one whose career Salton destroyed in revenge."

Karen nodded. "You're right, she seems like the perfect candidate. Unfortunately, she's vanished. She wasn't able to get a job after Salton screwed her over, and Stephanie doesn't know where she is now. Nor did the hospital personnel office. But like I said earlier, Zelen's a good cop. He'll find her soon enough."

CHAPTER 5

pulled into the MTRI parking lot just after eight the next morning, momentarily disturbing a downy woodpecker who was hunting for insects in one of the pine trees that surrounded the institute. A reminder of how much nicer it was to have a research lab here in Maine than in a big city like Boston. Then I went to my director's suite on the first floor where Anna, my administrative assistant, was waiting with a mug of coffee and a stack of papers. Although most of the institute's business was done by email—which I'd kept up with while I was in Boston—there was still a constant flow of routine paperwork, and I now had a week's accumulation to deal with.

I asked Anna to see if Stan Jacobs, our clinical director, could come by around eleven. Then I proceeded into my office and started going through Anna's stack. It didn't take long to see that there was nothing urgent, just routine administrative memos that needed my signoff, and I was nearly halfway through when I looked at my computer to find a new email that grabbed my attention.

Hi Brad, and welcome back. My new results look really good! I'm sure you're swamped on your first day, but I'll be in the lab if you have a chance to come by and go over the data. Ginger

I broke into a big grin. This was a helluva lot more exciting than routine administration. Ginger was one of two postdoctoral fellows who, along with seven graduate students and a technician, comprised my research group. She'd joined my lab a little over a year ago, after receiving her PhD in biochemistry from Boston University. Her thesis research had dealt with the mechanism of action of several drugs used in cancer treatment, and she now wanted to work directly on drug development. As she put it during her interview with me, she'd seen the devastating effects of cancer firsthand, and she wanted to do something to help people suffering from that horrible disease.

I'd been impressed with her record even before I met her. She'd published three very nice papers as a PhD student and had an exceptionally strong recommendation from her graduate adviser, Dan Crawford, who referred to her as "one of the very best students I've been privileged to train." I knew Dan, and he didn't say things like that lightly.

Her intelligence and drive were immediately apparent when I interviewed her. Moreover, she had a sound perspective on the current state of cancer research and was enthusiastic when we talked about the possible projects she could work on if she joined my lab. After spending an hour with her, I offered her a position and was delighted when she promptly accepted.

It didn't take long for her to prove that my judgment was correct. She was smart, good in the lab, and totally dedicated. I was hardworking myself, and my dual responsibilities as institute director and head of an active research lab often had me working weekends and long hours. But whenever I was in the institute, Ginger was there too. I once asked her jokingly if she ever took a day off.

"I can't afford to take time off," she replied seriously. "Do you realize that cancer kills more than ten people every minute in this country alone? How can I take a break when my work could save so many lives?"

Her intensity startled me, even scared me a bit, and I started to say that she couldn't take personal responsibility for the disease. But then she smiled, and I figured she'd been joking. At least I hoped so.

In any case, Ginger's combination of intelligence and dedication made her an incredible powerhouse. Her research had moved rapidly and met with dramatic success. The experiments that she'd said in her email "looked really good" were the final piece of a project that I thought represented a highly significant advance in treatment strategy.

I couldn't wait to go down to the lab and see her new results, but I knew I should stay in the office long enough to deal with the rest of Anna's stack and talk to Stan Jacobs. *Discipline.* I dashed off a quick email to Ginger saying that I was eager to see the data and would have time this afternoon. Then I forced myself to return to administrative memos.

I'd almost made it through the stack when Stan arrived shortly before eleven, dressed as usual in a slightly wrinkled shirt and jeans. I used to think his attire was oddly informal for the institute's clinical director, but I'd gotten accustomed to it. After all, this was Maine.

When we were seated at my conference table, I asked if he'd heard about Eric Salton.

"I know he got a big award at the meeting, but I haven't heard anything else. How'd your breakfast with him go?"

I wasn't sure how to tell him, so I went with simple and straightforward. "It didn't. He was killed the night before we planned to meet. Murdered in his hotel room."

Stan's mouth gaped open, and he sat rigidly upright. "Jesus! That's awful. What happened?"

"The cops are still working on it, but the detective in charge of the case is a friend of Karen's, so he filled us in. It looks like he was knifed by a woman who picked him up in the hotel lobby. They think it might have been a former student that he became involved with."

"Jesus," Stan said again. "He had an unsavory reputation for getting involved with students, but to get killed like that. What a terrible thing. Did you know him well?"

"No, just professionally. And as you're aware, I was hoping to get him interested in collaborating with us on some of the clinical trials we need to run."

"Which was a great idea. And now this." Stan sighed. "Have you thought about what to do instead? About the trials, I mean."

"Only that I'd start by talking to you about it."

He smiled faintly. "Okay, I'm always happy to be your sounding board. I know we have several promising new drugs under development, but how many are you thinking will be ready to start trials soon?"

"My understanding is that there are likely to be two candidates ready in the next month or so," I said. "The first is a new combination therapy for brain tumors that Tim Blanchard's developed. The second is a novel gene-targeted drug that Carolyn Gelman's been working on. Do you have the capacity to set up trials for those two here?"

"I'd like to, of course. But as you know, our clinic can't handle much more than what we already have going. I know about Tim's work, and we could probably manage that one. It's a new combination of two drugs that are already known to be active individually, so the trial would be small and well-defined. But I'm not familiar with what Carolyn has. Can you fill me in?"

"It's a novel drug against the *RAS* genes that are involved in a variety of different types of tumors. She designed it using the new artificial intelligence techniques, and I understand that the preclinical data they have with both cultured cells and tumors in mice are quite good."

"Knowing Carolyn, I don't doubt it," Stan remarked. "But evaluating a new drug like that is going to mean a larger trial than we'll need for Tim's combination. That's probably more than we can accommodate with everything else going on."

"I was afraid of that. Any ideas?"

"Actually, yes. Do you know Steve Lowell at Maine Med in Portland?" I shook my head, and Stan continued. "He's a good guy; I've known him since we were residents together at Mass General in Boston. More to the point, he's managed lots of clinical trials and has been intrigued by the *RAS* genes since they were first identified back in the eighties. Carolyn's drug might be something that would turn him on."

"Sounds promising. How do you think we should approach him? Since you know him, would it be best for you to make the initial contact?" I suggested.

"That probably makes sense, and I'd be happy to give him a call. But I don't know anything about Carolyn's project beyond what you just told me, and Steve's going to want to know the full story. Maybe you and I should call him together."

"We could, but if you think he'd really like to get the full picture, why don't we invite him down to visit the institute and give a seminar? That way he'd have a chance to meet with Carolyn and see the preclinical data firsthand."

Stan smiled. "I like that. And there's another thing about Steve that makes it an appealing idea. He's very big on communication with the general public. In fact, he's recently published a layman's book on cancer in which he spends a lot of time talking about how new drugs are developed, tested, and ultimately approved. I bet he wouldn't be able to resist an invitation to give a lecture that was open to the community."

"That'd be great! Sponsoring public events like that is a good community relations thing for the institute to do, and if you think Steve would like to give an open lecture, it sounds perfect. We can have his talk in the early evening so people will be able to come after work. He can meet with Carolyn and her group, as well as with you and anyone else he'd like to talk to, either earlier that day or the next. And I'll be happy to take him to dinner with you, or however else you'd like me to be involved."

To my surprise, Stan was hesitant. "That sounds good, but do you think people from outside the institute will actually come to an evening lecture? I'm worried that we could just wind up embarrassing ourselves if nobody shows up."

I winked at him. "That'd certainly be embarrassing. But think for a minute. How do we get students to come to seminars?"

He looked blank for a moment. Then he got it. "We have pizza for them afterward. Is that your plan here?"

"Something like that. I'm thinking of a reception after the lecture with wine and plenty of high-end goodies. Steve can sign copies of his book, which any author would love, and we'll advertise it in conjunction with the Wells and York public libraries as an author talk. As well as running a couple of announcements in the local newspaper."

Stan grinned. "So a more sophisticated version of pizza for the students. You're right, that'll bring out the crowds. And Steve will be in seventh heaven. But how're you going to pay for a bash like that? Is there some secret entertainment stash in the institute budget that you're keeping from the rest of us?"

"Don't worry, it won't cost us a thing. The trustees love that kind of community outreach. I won't have any trouble getting them to cough up whatever funding we need to make a splash."

Stan inclined his head. "I guess that's your magic touch as director. Okay, I'll call Steve and see what I can set up. And good luck with your deep-pocket trustee friends."

After Stan left, I forced myself to finish off the remainder of the administrative correspondence Anna had handed me. That done, I checked my email to see what else had come in and was surprised to find a message from Stan.

Talked to Steve. He's excited about coming for a visit and giving a public talk. Would three weeks from now work for you? I already checked with Carolyn, and she's available.

I sent a quick reply, copying Anna so she could put it on the calendar and be prepared to work with Stan on the arrangements.

Great! Please go ahead. Anna can help you set it up, and I'm looking forward to it.

Then I headed down to my lab for the fun part of the day: meeting with Ginger.

CHAPTER 6

When Ginger first joined the lab, we decided on a project designed to target drugs selectively to cancer cells. The standard drugs used in chemotherapy all have a common shortcoming. They aren't specific for cancer cells. They also kill patients' normal cells, which limits how much of the drug patients can tolerate and, in many cases, precludes effective treatment.

An important new approach to this problem had been developed recently by coupling drugs to antibodies that recognize markers on the surface of cancer cells. These so-called antibody-drug conjugates or ADCs deliver the drugs efficiently and selectively to cancer cells while sparing normal cells. You could think of treating patients with ADCs as being akin to using guided missiles to convey drugs specifically to their target.

Although some of these ADCs worked remarkably well, there were still many patients whose cancers failed to respond. We decided to see if this could be improved by coupling a drug to two different antibodies, recognizing two distinct cancer cell markers, rather than to just one. The idea was that, even if a cancer cell wasn't recognized by one of the two antibodies, the other would still let it serve as a target.

We chose markers that are frequently present on lung cancer cells, and Ginger initiated a series of experiments to test the effectiveness of ADCs directed against two such markers. Her initial studies on cells growing in culture were promising, and she went on to do experiments with tumors in mice that had been produced by lung cancer cell lines. Her results were a dramatic success, with thirteen out of fifteen lung cancer cell lines responding significantly better to the double-antibody ADC than to either of the single-antibody ADCs alone.

We could have stopped there and published the results, but we decided to take the project one step further. Although cancer cell lines like we'd used were commonly employed for drug testing, they often gave results that didn't accurately reflect the activity of a drug against real tumors in patients. The problem was that cell lines maintained in the laboratory changed over time, gradually differing in important characteristics from the tumors from which they'd originated.

One way of addressing this shortcoming was to test drugs against tumors that had been generated by transplanting pieces of a human tumor directly into mice. These explanted tumors could be transplanted from one mouse to another while maintaining the characteristics of the human tumors from which they'd been derived. Most importantly for us, they'd been shown in several studies to yield drug-screening results that were similar to the responses of the original human tumors.

Although explanted tumors were much harder to work with than cultured cell lines, they were clearly a better model, so we obtained explants from the tumors of ten different lung cancer patients. Ginger then treated mice bearing tumors from each of the explants with her new double-antibody ADC and compared the response to treatment with each of the single-antibody ADCs alone, similar to the experiments she'd done with tumors derived from cell lines.

And now she had the results!

I spotted Ginger's shoulder-length chestnut hair as soon as I entered my lab. She was at her desk in the back, facing away from me. Most of my other students were at their desks and lab benches that jutted out of the wall perpendicular to the windowed side of the lab, so I passed by them while I went to see Ginger. I couldn't very well just hurry past after having been away for a week, so I stopped and chatted briefly with each of them on my way to the back of the room.

Since I had to make several stops, the trip took a while, and Ginger heard me as I progressed slowly to where she was sitting. By the time I reached her, she was watching me with a mischievous smile.

"Glad you finally made it back here, Professor," she teased. "I don't suppose you'd like to see the explanted tumor results, would you?"

I responded in kind. "Oh, I don't know. You already told me they were pretty good. I probably don't need to look at the data."

We both laughed, enjoying the joke for a minute. Then she turned serious, although there was still a distinct glint of pleasure in her light brown eyes. I took a seat next to her, and she opened her notebook so we could look at the results together.

For each of the ten explanted tumors, she'd plotted tumor growth without any treatment, after treatment with her double-antibody ADC, and after treatment with each of the two single-antibody ADCs separately. The results were even more dramatic than those she'd obtained with cell lines.

The growth of tumors from eight of the ten patient explants was inhibited by the double-antibody ADC. Not only that, the tumors from six of them were completely eliminated. In contrast, the two single-antibody ADCs each inhibited the growth of only four explanted tumors, and only completely eliminated tumors from two of them.

"What do you think?" she asked with a grin. "The single-antibody ADCs work about as well on the explants as they do in real patients."

I interrupted and finished her thought. "And your double-antibody ADC is one helluva lot better. A response rate of eighty percent versus forty percent with the singles, and what looks like a complete remission rate of sixty percent versus twenty percent. Ginger, this is nothing short of spectacular!"

Her smile morphed into an ear-to-ear grin. "It really is nice, isn't it? I've hardly been able to wait to show you these results."

"They're beautiful. With these data, your paper is going to be a complete blow-away. And if the double-antibody ADC works like this is in the clinic, your results are going to save lives."

At that, she jumped up and threw her arms around me. "Oh, Brad, that's so great! Thank you for getting me on this project. To think that it might make a difference for real patients is just . . . I don't know. I'm so excited I can't even think what to say."

I gently extricated myself from her hug. No matter how innocent, physical contact with a student or postdoc wasn't a good idea. But I fully understood her excitement.

"Why don't you treat yourself to a celebration tonight?" I suggested. "A fancy dinner with your favorite person, or whatever you most enjoy. Then tomorrow let's put our heads together and start working on the paper. These results are important enough to make a big splash, so what do you think about sending it to *Natural Science and Medicine*?"

Natural Science and Medicine was the top journal in the field, and having a paper published there would be a big boost to Ginger's career. I expected her to be thrilled at the idea, but she surprised me with an unenthusiastic response. Maybe she was being cautious.

"If that's where you think we should send it, it's fine with me.

I'll get started writing, and I'm happy to submit the paper wherever you want. But in the meantime, what do you think I should do next in the lab?"

"Your new results seem like a good stopping point for the current phase, so let's get the paper written up first. That'll let us see if there are any holes we need to plug, and then we can talk about where to go experimentally."

"No problem, I'll start on the paper right away. But I can work in the lab at the same time. You said that my results could be important for how patients are treated. I know we need to publish a paper, but beyond that, what do we need to do to turn the double-antibody approach into a real treatment? Should I do experiments with tumor explants from additional patients?"

I shrugged my shoulders. "That might be something the reviewers will ask for, but the results you have are so clear-cut that I don't think more patient explants are needed before we submit. Just imagine if you were one of the patients whose tumor explant was wiped out by the double-antibody ADC! As far as I'm concerned, we're ready to take it to the next step: a clinical trial so we can see if it works in real patients."

Now her eyes glowed with the excitement that had been missing when I talked about sending her paper to *Natural Science and Medicine.* She really was that unusual postdoc who was more focused on the real-world impact of her work than on advancing her career. She'd said as much back when I'd interviewed her for the position, and I needed to keep her priorities in mind.

"That's great, Brad. You know helping patients is what I really want to do," she gushed. "How do we get a clinical trial started?"

I smiled. "I love your enthusiasm. We'll need to collaborate with a physician to run a trial, ideally someone who has experience in the area. And to do that, we'll have to convince them that your results merit moving forward to patients, so the first thing you'll need to do is to get that paper written up. Once everything's together, and hopefully through at least the first round of review at

Natural Science and Medicine, I'll start approaching potential clinical collaborators."

Ginger started to say something, but another voice broke in. "And just how are you planning to do that, Brad?"

I turned to find Carolyn Gelman standing behind us.

CHAPTER 7

Carolyn was my closest friend and colleague at the institute, so I didn't mind the interruption. But I couldn't resist teasing her. "Do you always sneak up on people to eavesdrop?"

She laughed. "Whenever I have the chance. But seriously, I just stopped by to ask about a conversation I had with Stan Jacobs, and I didn't want to interrupt you mid-sentence." Turning to Ginger, she added, "I did hear enough to get the idea that you have some exciting new results. Congratulations!"

"She certainly does," I agreed. "Ginger, why don't you show Carolyn your new data?"

Ginger looked like she was about to purr with delight. "Of course, I'd love to!"

I got up so Carolyn could sit next to her, and Ginger went through her tumor explant results. I could see the excitement growing on Carolyn's face as she watched the data unfold. It didn't take long for her to get it.

"Wow," she burst out, "this is really amazing! Congratulations to both of you! And Brad, I think what you were saying is absolutely right. With these results, you're ready to take it to the clinic."

I squeezed Ginger's shoulder as I replied. "Thanks, Carolyn. You've had drugs go through clinical trials before, so I'm glad to hear you say that. But that's not why you're here. What did you want to see me about?"

"After I talked to Stan, I had a thought on the schedule for Steve Lowell's visit that I wanted to run by you."

Ginger started to get up and excuse herself while Carolyn and I talked, but I stopped her.

"Hold on, Ginger. You should hear about this. Lowell's visit might be a good opportunity to present your story to a doc who runs clinical trials."

"Absolutely," Carolyn agreed. "That fits right in with what I was going to suggest."

I turned to Ginger and filled her in. "Lowell is a clinician at Maine Med in Portland who's run lots of clinical trials. Stan Jacobs knows him and thinks he might be interested in working with Carolyn on a new drug she's developed, so we're inviting him down to give a lecture and hear what Carolyn has. And now I'm wondering if we should also talk to him about your double-antibody ADC while he's here."

Carolyn jumped in as a vigorous second. "You definitely should. I've interacted with him at a couple of conferences, and he's a good guy. I think you'd like working with him, and I'm sure he'd flip out at Ginger's data."

"Do you think he'd be able to set up trials for both your new drug and our ADCs?" I asked. "I don't want us to get in your way."

Carolyn waved a hand dismissively. "Don't worry about it. Steve has a big operation, and I'm sure he wouldn't have any problem working on both our projects. In fact, I think he'd welcome the opportunity."

"Okay then. Ginger, how's that sound to you?"

"Fabulous! My God, I can't believe how fast this is happening!"

"You're right, it is fast. His visit is only three weeks from now. Do you think you can have all your data together and a paper in shape by then?"

"Are you kidding? I'll have it all done in three *days* if you need it!"

I laughed. "Okay tiger, I'll have Stan add us to the schedule."

Then I turned back to Carolyn and winked. "Now that you've gotten us started on the road to a clinical trial, should we get back to whatever it is you came to talk about?"

"I don't know, helping to get you and Ginger on course might be enough for me. But my question wasn't entirely unrelated. Are you thinking that both you and Ginger will meet with Steve when he's here?"

"Sure, why not? Ginger, you'd like to be involved in that meeting, wouldn't you?"

By now, Ginger was flushed with excitement. "Oh, yes! I'd love to be part of it."

"So that was my question," Carolyn broke in. "I'm sure my students would like to be involved too, but Stan was thinking of just having me meet with Steve. Would it be okay with you to make it more inclusive?"

"Of course. Your students should have every opportunity to be part of the conversation. Who in your lab has worked on the project?"

"Barbara Slotkin and Penny Alberts. They're both fourth-year graduate students. Barbara did the initial AI work to design the drug with our computational collaborator, and then she and Penny worked together on testing it out."

"I know Barbara," Ginger chimed in. "She's really good with computer stuff. I can see her doing the drug design part."

"Do you think Steve would be interested in hearing about that part of the project, in addition to the drug testing results?" I asked Carolyn.

"Knowing Steve, I'm sure he would. He's been interested in

RAS genes for years and will be intrigued by how we designed a new inhibitor. What I'd actually like to do is to have Barbara present that part of the work and then have Penny present the testing data, rather than just have me do all the talking. I think that would be fairer to the students, as well as more interesting for Steve."

"Absolutely," I agreed. "Ginger, sound okay to you?"

She grinned and nodded vigorously. "Definitely!"

Then I had another idea. "You know, why don't we make it a joint session? A little mini-symposium where first you guys could present, then Ginger could go through her data, and then we'd all have a chance to discuss strategies for moving forward with Steve. Carolyn, you know him. Do you think he'd enjoy a session like that?"

Her response was unequivocal. "He'd absolutely love it. I'll talk to Stan and set it up."

CHAPTER 8

I was uncertain about how my first day back to work would unfold, so Karen and I hadn't made plans for dinner. I figured we'd probably get takeout but was pleasantly surprised when she called and suggested that we go to our favorite sushi place instead. It was a pleasant spring evening, and the owner welcomed dogs on his outside patio, so she offered to stop at home and pick up Rosie. All I had to do was meet them at the restaurant.

Ogunquit, an Abenaki word meaning "beautiful place by the sea," was immediately south of Wells on the coast. It had been part of Wells until 1980, when it seceded and incorporated as a small town with an area of four-square miles and a population of less than sixteen hundred year-round residents. But Ogunquit was a popular summer tourist destination—known for its beautiful beaches, large LGBTQ population, and summer theater—and it was flooded with over fifty thousand visitors between Memorial Day and Labor Day.

Happily, the summer influx hadn't started yet, and the restaurant had just opened for the season. I got there to find Karen sitting at one of the half-dozen outdoor tables on Main Street, sipping sake from a small cup. Rosie lay underneath the table next to her water bowl, the picture of a contented pug out for dinner with her people.

Karen started to pour sake for me as I kissed her and sat down, but I held up a hand to stop her. "Thanks, but hot sake's not my favorite. I'm going to get a scotch instead."

"I know you don't usually like it but give this a try. The owner suggested it when he came over to give Rosie a special treat. It's some of the really good stuff, served chilled rather than warm."

"In that case, I'll have to check it out." I took a sip and was surprised at how good it was. "You're right, this goes down beautifully." Raising my cup, I made the Japanese toast, "Kampai."

"I thought you'd like it. They're pretty busy tonight, so I went ahead and ordered our usual selection. And a little plain broiled fish for Rosie."

Just then, the waiter arrived with dinner. He put a large platter of sushi on the table and ceremoniously bowed as he reached underneath to give Rosie a small plate of cooked fish. Rosie accepted the tribute with less formality but attacked her plate with lip smacks and slurping noises that made her appreciation clear.

In the meantime, Karen started in on the sushi, beginning, of course, with her favorite, the house special lobster roll—a lobster and avocado roll that was topped with a double portion of lobster. I left that to her, at least for the moment, and used my chopsticks to select a piece of yellowtail nigiri and dip it in soy sauce. Then I asked how her day had gone.

She paused only momentarily on her way to grabbing a second piece of the lobster roll. "Nothing traumatic. Tell me about yours first."

I suppressed a laugh. That was exactly the response I'd expected. Karen liked to concentrate on her food, not talk while she ate. Especially with an appealing assortment like this in front of her.

She proceeded with her demolition of dinner while I told her about Ginger's results, managing to pause just long enough to say, "That's great!"

Then I went on to tell her about Stan's suggestion of Steve Lowell as a collaborator for our clinical trials and the plans we'd made for his visit. By the time I finished, she was slowing down enough to talk, having polished off all but one piece of the lobster roll and a good part of the rest of our dinner.

"Sounds like you had quite a nice return to work. Good data and a potential replacement for Eric Salton in the works. But aren't you hungry? You better stop talking and have some sushi before I eat it all."

This time I didn't hide my amusement. "Well, you had me talking while you were eating. Now maybe we can switch, and you can tell me about your day. Or should we order more sushi first?"

She grinned. "Sorry, you know how I am with a nice platter of this stuff. But I'm set now. And there is something that I want to talk to you about."

I started to reach for the remaining piece of lobster roll but noticed that Karen was looking at it longingly. So I diverted my chopsticks toward a piece of salmon nigiri. "Sure you don't want that last piece of lobster roll? It has your name on it."

She hesitated, but only for a moment. Then she gave me a wink and grabbed it. "Okay, twist my arm. But this is my last piece."

There was a plentiful selection of goodies left, so I proceeded to enjoy myself while Karen finished her lobster roll and took over the conversation.

"Everything was pretty well in hand at the unit. Just some petty nuisance stuff happened while I was away, nothing big. But I got an interesting call from Zelen."

"Does he have something new on Salton's murder?"

"Looks like it. He's located the woman whose career Salton destroyed when she resisted his advances. She's now working in a small primary care practice in Damariscotta."

"That's quite a step down from where she was headed as a clinical oncology fellow with Salton," I noted. "He must have done quite a number on her."

"I suspect so. She's also gone back to using her maiden name, Claire Weinstein. She was married and used the name of Casper as a fellow."

"Sounds like she may have needed to hide her history with Salton. Which no doubt means she has plenty of motive for revenge. But if she's not involved in oncology anymore, it doesn't seem likely that she would have been at the cancer research meeting in Boston."

Karen shrugged. "Maybe not. But Zelen checked, and she was a registered attendee. Not only that, there's security video of her in the lecture hall the evening Salton was killed."

I drained my sake cup and poured another as I took that in. "So she had both motive and opportunity. What's Zelen's next move?"

"He wants to question her and get a DNA sample to compare with the crime scene. I'm going to meet him in Damariscotta tomorrow, in case he needs someone from Maine there."

"Because he can't make an out-of-state arrest?" I asked.

"Right. And he'd also like you to come, if you can get away from MTRI for another day."

I sat up with a jolt. "Me! What's he want me there for?"

Karen shrugged her shoulders and smiled. "That was my reaction, too. He said it might be useful to have your help in understanding both her career path and whatever explanation she offers for having attended the cancer meeting. But I think maybe he just likes your company."

CHAPTER 9

We took my car for the eighty-mile trip to Damariscotta, heading north on I-95 and I-295 through Portland and Freeport, and then east on US 1 along the coast. Just before we crossed the Sheepscot River in Wiscasset, Karen cried out so loudly that I was afraid I was about to hit something. "Look! Red's Eats is open!"

I rolled my eyes. "You just had lobster sushi last night. You can't be ready for lobster again."

"C'mon, it's totally different. Red's is the best place for lobster rolls in all of Maine. Let's stop. The line's not even too long, not like the hour wait we had last summer."

I looked at my watch. "We're already late for meeting Zelen and we're still at least ten minutes away. How about waiting until we come back to hit Red's?"

She gave a disappointed sigh. "I suppose you're right. Well okay, as long as we stop on the way home. No matter what!"

I knew better than to argue, so I promised we would as we crossed the river and proceeded to Damariscotta. Google maps directed us to a small building just off Main Street, and Zelen's car was parked in front when we got there. A sign above the door was inscribed "Damariscotta Primary Care" and listed Claire Weinstein MD along with two other physicians.

Two patients were sitting on well-worn faux leather chairs in the waiting room. A similarly upholstered three-seat couch was across from them, and a receptionist was stationed behind a glass window at the back of the room. We went up to her, and Karen said that we needed to see Dr. Weinstein. When the woman replied that Dr. Weinstein was fully booked, Karen held up her ID.

"This is official police business. Is she in her office?"

The receptionist blanched. "I'm sorry, she's with a patient. She should be just finishing up; can you wait until then?"

Karen looked at Zelen, who shrugged, and Karen told the receptionist we'd wait. A few minutes later, a patient came out, and the receptionist picked up her phone. "I'll let her know you're here."

"That's all right," Zelen interrupted. "We'll just go ahead back to her office."

We proceeded down a hall behind the reception desk. There were four exam rooms, a restroom, and three offices with physician's names on their doors. The second was Claire Weinstein's.

Karen knocked on the door, and we went in without waiting for a response. A severe-looking woman with short black hair and silver-framed glasses was sitting behind an inexpensive wooden desk. From her history, I figured Claire Weinstein was in her mid-thirties, but her lined face and tired eyes made her appear ten years older.

When Karen held up her ID and asked if she was Claire Weinstein, her annoyance was undisguised. "I'm *Dr.* Weinstein, yes. And I don't appreciate your barging in here without an appointment. I have a full schedule, and you should know I can't discuss anything related to my patients. What is it you want?"

"We have a few questions for you. Nothing concerning your patients, don't worry about confidentiality. I'm Lieutenant Richmond, Maine State Police. This is Detective Zelen from the Boston PD, and our colleague Dr. Parker."

Now that Karen had introduced us, Zelen took over. "To start with, I'm curious as to how you wound up in private practice as a primary care physician. I believe your training was in oncology, wasn't it?"

"What the hell does that have to do with anything?" Weinstein bristled.

"We need you to answer our questions," Karen told her. "This'll be quicker if you cooperate."

Weinstein sighed resignedly. "All right, fine. That's correct, I was in oncology. But I decided I didn't like it. This is a better fit."

"I see." Zelen consulted his notebook. "And you made that decision after completing a three-year fellowship with Eric Salton at the Mass General Cancer Center, is that right?"

"Yes, that's right." Her brow furrowed. "What's this all about?"

Rather than letting Zelen answer, Karen broke in. "How did you find Salton as a mentor? Was he good to work with?"

Weinstein shrugged. "He was okay. Very smart and dedicated. And he has lots of connections. Is this about Eric?"

She seemed interested in our visit for the first time, which made me wonder if she thought we were investigating Salton. If so, I figured I knew how to get her to open up.

"I'm in cancer research myself," I said. "We've thought about setting up a collaboration with Salton, but I've heard concerns about the way he relates to the women he works with. Talk of sexual harassment, in fact. Is there anything to that?"

It worked. My question opened a floodgate. "Damn right there is! The evil bastard. The truth is, it's his fault that I wound up here. He hit on me when I was a second-year fellow. I turned him down, but he wouldn't take no for an answer. He only stopped after I threatened to report him, and then he destroyed my career in revenge."

I wasn't surprised when Karen sighed and responded sympathetically. "That's horrible, I'm so sorry. Can you tell us more about what he did?"

Weinstein nodded, fully cooperative now. "I hope you can put him away for the things he's done. I'm not his only victim, and jail's too good for him. He stopped propositioning me after I threatened to report him, but he went on a crusade to ruin me professionally instead. The first thing he did was to stop interacting with me in the lab and cut me out of the interesting projects. I thought about leaving, but I'd already been there for almost two years and starting over somewhere else didn't seem to make sense. So I stuck it out and completed the fellowship. I thought that I'd be free of him after that, but that's when he really went after me."

"What happened?" Karen prompted.

"I started looking for an academic oncology job in Boston, but none of the places I applied to even invited me for an interview. After a few months, I figured that Eric knew those were the places I'd be interested in and used his connections to blackball me. So I started looking outside of Boston, applying to places I didn't think Eric would reach out to. I finally started getting interviews, but still no job offers. Finally, someone anonymously sent me a copy of the 'recommendation' letter Eric had written, I guess because they felt sorry for me. It basically said I was incompetent and possibly a fraud, which, of course, ensured that no one would ever hire me. After that I realized that I needed to forget about oncology and just delete my fellowship with Eric from my CV. That meant a job like this in general practice was the only possibility, but at least it was something. I was still afraid Eric could interfere, so I switched to using my maiden name in hopes that he wouldn't be able to find me."

It was a horrible story, and I felt awful for her. Karen looked stricken, no doubt remembering a similar dark time when she'd suffered from harassment as a detective with the Boston police. I thought she was about to say something, but Zelen spoke first.

"That's terrible," he said sympathetically. "You must hate him for what he did to you."

She made a sarcastic snorting sound. "You think? I'd like to kill the bastard. Although I'll settle for helping you guys put him away."

Zelen nodded. "I can understand why. But I have to ask, where were you three evenings ago? April twenty-seventh."

I suspected his sympathy for her was real. He was fundamentally a decent guy. But he was also a cop with a killer to catch.

Her eyes widened. And then her face hardened with suspicion. "I was home, like always. What's this about? You aren't going after Eric, are you?"

"Is there anybody who can confirm you were home that night?" Karen asked.

"No. I'm divorced and live alone." She gave a bitter laugh. "My marriage was another casualty of Salton's harassment."

"So you didn't go to the American Association for Cancer Research meeting in Boston?" Zelen asked. "Every though you were a registered participant?"

She licked her lips nervously. "No. I wasn't feeling well so I stayed home that night."

Now Zelen held up his phone. "Is this you?"

"I . . . I guess so. It looks like me."

"It's from a security camera in the meeting's auditorium. Taken shortly before Eric Salton gave an award lecture. And roughly three hours before he was murdered in his hotel room. Do you have anything you want to tell us about that?"

CHAPTER 10

"Murdered!" Claire Weinstein exclaimed. "Somebody finally killed the lousy bastard. I hope he suffered. But it wasn't me, if that's what you're thinking."

"It's a little hard for us to just accept that," Zelen replied. "You hated him, albeit for good reason. And you were there at the time he was murdered."

"Which you just lied to us about," Karen added. "If you didn't go to the meeting to kill Salton, why were you there?"

"I wanted to hear about the newest developments. I spent years working on cancer, and I'm still interested in the field. Even though Salton forced me out."

Possible, I thought. Unless it was another lie. "That's admirable," I said. "I was there too. Do you remember Dr. French's talk on his new breast cancer treatment? I thought that was really impressive."

"I agree," she responded enthusiastically. "It's a significant advance."

I exhaled slowly. "Except there was no such talk and no Dr. French. Is there anything from the meeting that you *do* remember?"

"You bastard, you tricked me! All right, fine. I didn't care about the damn meeting; I just went to Salton's talk because I wanted to heckle him. I was going to embarrass him during the question period by calling him out as a harasser. But I couldn't bring myself to do it in front of all those people in the audience, so I just left."

Zelen got up and stood over her. "Bullshit! I think you went there to kill him. You disguised yourself with a blond wig, came on to him in the hotel after his talk, and butchered him when he took you back to his room."

"No! He deserved killing, but I didn't do it."

Zelen grunted. "After all the lies you've told us, you'll forgive me if I don't believe you."

"That's your problem, asshole. You don't have any evidence, just supposition."

At that Karen spoke up. "We have motive and opportunity, which is enough for me to arrest you. But you could establish your innocence here and now by agreeing to a DNA test. We got samples of the killer's DNA from the hotel room, and its profile is already in CODIS, the FBI database. If we had a sample of your DNA, we could do a rapid analysis right here with a portable device Detective Zelen has in his car. It would only take about an hour, and you could go about your day while we wait outside for the results. We just need a mouth swab."

Weinstein's reply was as quick as it was angry. "Screw you! You set this whole thing up to get me to talk about Eric. I'm not letting you take a DNA sample; you'd just use it to frame me. Get the hell out of my office!"

Karen shook her head. "That's not one of the options. You either let us take a sample voluntarily, or we arrest you and take a sample at the station during booking."

"Fuck off! I'm calling my lawyer."

She started to reach for her phone, but Karen pulled out a pair of handcuffs. "As you wish. Claire Weinstein, I'm placing you under arrest for the murder of Eric Salton. Stand up and put your hands behind your back. You can call your lawyer from the station after you're booked."

Instead of complying, she jumped up and tried to shove Karen aside. It was a stupid move. Karen grabbed her arm, twisted it behind her back, and pinned her against the desk.

That seemed to make her finally realize that she didn't have much choice. "All right, wait! Go ahead and take your goddamned DNA."

Karen looked at her skeptically for a moment. Then she agreed. "Okay. But if you try any more funny moves, I'm going to take you in for resisting arrest whatever the DNA results say."

But Weinstein had apparently had enough and let Zelen swab her mouth. Then Karen told her that we'd be back when we got the results, and we left her in the office.

CHAPTER 11

As soon as we were out in the hall, Zelen stopped and turned to Karen. "I think she's going to try to run. She's guilty as hell, or she'd have let us get her DNA in the beginning. When she saw it was inevitable, I think she decided there was a better chance to get away from here than she'd have if we took her in."

"You could be right," Karen agreed. "Although it's possible that she just lost control and then thought better of it. Anyway, I can see an exit down the hall leading to the back of the building. One of us should cover that while the other waits out front."

Zelen nodded. "I need to get the sample into my analyzer, which is out front in the car. Why don't I go do that and cover the front, while you take the back? I'll let you know when the results come in, on the off-chance that she doesn't make her play before then."

Karen and I went out through the back exit. A quick survey of the building established that it was the only way out besides the front door, so we found a nearby bench and waited.

I didn't know what to think. I couldn't help but sympathize

with Claire Weinstein after what Salton had done to her. Part of me hoped she was innocent and had just been shaken up by a visit from the cops. On the other hand, everything pointed to her, and I more than half expected her to come sneaking out the back at any moment.

When Zelen came around the side of the building and waved, I assumed that we'd found our killer.

But to my surprise, he shook his head. "No match. It ain't her."

I didn't anticipate how relieved I'd feel at that news. After what Salton had done to her, I didn't want it to be Claire Weinstein. Karen must have felt the same, because she immediately got up and said, "Good. Let's go tell her."

We went in through the back door and found Weinstein in her office. She sat up rigidly straight and her eyes filled with fear when we entered—she really was afraid that we'd faked the DNA results to frame her. But Karen was quick to give her the news.

"Relax. The DNA proves that you didn't kill him. I'm sorry we had to put you through this. And even more sorry for what he did to you."

She sank back into her chair. "Thank you. Is there anything else?"

Zelen cleared his throat. "Just two more questions. Do you know the names of any other former students that he harassed? And did you see anyone you recognized at his lecture that night?"

Weinstein glared at him. "No and no. But do you seriously think I'd help you find his killer? If I knew who it was, I'd give them a fucking medal."

Zelen started to say something, but Karen put a hand on his arm and shook her head. "She's been through enough. Let's go."

We left the office. But Karen turned back, went over to Weinstein, and gave her a hug. I couldn't hear what she said, but it made Weinstein smile for the first time since we'd confronted her.

———

Neither Karen nor I said anything after we left Zelen and started home. We were used to compatible silence, so it wasn't uncomfortable to be together but at the same time alone with our thoughts. I finally spoke when we crossed the Sheepscot River and Red's Eats loomed on our right. "Ready for the lobster roll stop you made me promise?"

She turned to me with a faint smile that didn't reach her eyes. "Thanks for remembering, but I don't want anything now. We can stop if you want to, or else we can just pick something up when we get home."

So, she was too upset by the afternoon's events to even want lobster. I wasn't surprised. The commonalities between what Salton had done to Claire Weinstein and what Karen herself had suffered early in her career were striking.

She'd told me the story years ago, shortly after we first met. I was a department chair at Boston Technological Institute, and Karen was a university detective, assigned to work with me on a case of sexual harassment in my department. I'd quickly been impressed with how efficient and insightful she was, which made me curious as to why she was a university cop instead of being with the city or state police.

When I asked, she told me that she'd planned to go to law school but decided to join the Boston PD after the attack of September eleventh. She'd been promoted to detective rapidly and made a name for herself by solving a major case. Then her lieutenant tried to force her to have sex with him. She'd refused, but he persisted, and eventually she filed a complaint. That wasn't something cops did back then, and her colleagues united against her when the lieutenant claimed that Karen was the one who tried to proposition him. She was forced to resign and then discovered that her former lieutenant's "reference" was preventing her from getting another job. Finally, the chief of the university police, who was female, listened to Karen's side of the story and decided to give her a chance.

She'd been happy in that position, until the case we were working on evolved into a murderous conspiracy that reached all the way up to the president of the university. When it broke to a flurry of publicity, she was offered a position as a special agent with the FBI. She enjoyed the excitement of the Bureau and transferred from Boston to the Portland office after I became director of MTRI. Three years ago, a high-level position in the Maine State Police became open, and she was recruited to her present post as commanding officer of one of Maine's three major crimes units.

I reached over and squeezed her arm. "You're thinking about the similarities between what you went through and what happened to Weinstein, aren't you?"

Karen sighed. "Her story brought back all the feelings I had back then, when it looked like everything I'd worked for had been destroyed by that asshole lieutenant. I had some lucky breaks and made it out of the pit, but I don't see how Weinstein's going to get beyond where she is now."

"I know. I hope she does, but I don't see a path forward for her. What'd you say to her when you went back and gave her a hug? It actually made her smile."

"I told her that if Zelen ever did find Salton's killer, I'd pin a medal on her too."

"You weren't just joking, were you?"

"You know I wasn't. Salton deliberately destroyed Claire Weinstein, his own student, just because she wouldn't have sex with him. He was a man who needed killing."

"Do you think Zelen will figure out who did it? It seemed like Weinstein was his only solid lead."

"I don't know. It's going to be tough for him to move forward from here. He didn't find any complaints against Salton in the personnel records, so he's going to have to work through the list of Salton's clinical fellows, hoping to find someone else who seems like a suspect."

I was skeptical. "Weinstein stood out because her career had been so dramatically disrupted that she couldn't even stay in oncology. But the killer wouldn't have to be somebody who suffered like she did. It could just as easily be someone who gave in to Salton but hated him for forcing her."

"I know," Karen said. "In which case, I don't know if Zelen will ever find somebody for me to pin that medal on."

CHAPTER 12

Zelen called Karen with occasional updates, but without much progress, for the next couple of weeks. He'd compiled a list of two dozen women who'd been clinical fellows with Salton over the last ten years and was working his way through it. Most had gone on to pursue careers in oncology, many at leading institutions. Those that he'd spoken to praised Salton as a mentor, insisting that they never heard rumors or been subjected to any kind of sexual misconduct. Which, of course, was what you'd expect them to say if they'd killed him and were being questioned by the police.

There were two, however, that Zelen thought might be promising. Like Claire Weinstein, they hadn't followed the expected career path after completing their fellowships. One had left clinical medicine altogether and gone into basic science. She was now an assistant professor at the University of Michigan, teaching cell biology and conducting research on the fundamental structure of cell membranes. The other had done a second fellowship in pathology and was working at a hospital in Virginia.

Zelen was planning to interview them after looking further into their backgrounds, including whatever recommendations they'd gotten from Salton. He'd also be talking to the remaining women on his list, as well as to the male fellows who'd worked with Salton, since they might also have information on women who'd been victimized. It would probably take a while, but he was committed to staying on the case and promised to keep Karen informed.

After our session with Claire Weinstein, Karen was more than happy to be left out of it. At least part of her didn't want to see Salton's killer caught, and she was relieved that none of Zelen's other suspects were in Maine, where she'd have to get involved.

As for me, I had my hands full at MTRI. In addition to the normal demands of research and my administrative responsibilities, I'd been hustling to get Ginger's work into shape for Steve Lowell's visit, which was now about to happen. If we expected him to seriously consider collaborating with us, I felt that we needed to present him with a completed manuscript that ideally had made it through the initial round of editorial review at *Natural Science and Medicine*. And Ginger had to have a top-notch presentation ready for the mini-symposium session we were planning with Carolyn's group.

Fortunately, Ginger was Ginger. Meaning that she was really good at writing up her results, just as she was at designing and performing experiments. She sent me a first draft of the paper just three days after she showed me her data with the explanted tumors. That was so fast that I didn't think the draft would be any good, but I was wrong. She'd pretty much nailed it on her first try. We spent a few days passing it back and forth for revisions, and then it was ready to submit.

I stuck to my initial plan and sent the paper to *Natural Science and Medicine*. It was important enough to merit publication in the field's top journal, even though I knew sending it there was risky. *Natural Science and Medicine* rejected most submissions out-of-hand, simply because the editors didn't consider them important enough. But I received an email with good news last week.

Dear Dr. Parker:

We have reviewed your paper, Increased Efficacy of Double-Anti-body ADCs for Lung Cancer Treatment, *and have decided that your work meets the high standard of significance required for publication in* Natural Science and Medicine. *Accordingly, the paper has been sent to outside reviewers who are experts in the field for detailed evaluation of the science as well as further input on the significance of the results. We will be in touch again with a decision after we have received their comments.*

Thank you for the opportunity to consider your work.

Jerome Blackwell, Editor

It wasn't final acceptance, of course, but this was exactly what I wanted to have on hand for Lowell's visit. While Ginger's data spoke for itself, an independent vote of confidence from the editor of *Natural Science and Medicine* couldn't help but pique his interest. Ginger and I had already been through two practice sessions of the oral presentation she'd be giving a little later this afternoon, and I had no doubt that she'd put on an impressive show.

In short, I was confident and ready when Anna knocked on the door and announced Steve Lowell's arrival.

I got up to greet him and indicated that we should sit at my conference table. Anna brought in coffee while we exchanged a few preliminaries and quickly reviewed the day's schedule. Then I turned to the principal purpose of his visit.

"I really appreciate your being willing to engage in the session Carolyn and I have planned with our students. I'm hoping it'll not only give you a chance to hear the full stories behind our new drugs, but also give the students a unique opportunity to get an inside view of how clinical trials work."

"I'm the one who's grateful to you for organizing this visit," Lowell responded graciously. "The session you've planned with the students sounds like fun. And the projects that both you and Carolyn have been working on look really interesting."

"I'm happy to be able to tell you that the editors of *Natural Science and Medicine* seem to think so too. We just heard that the manuscript I sent you earlier has passed the first round of editorial review."

"Excellent, congratulations. The *Natural Science and Medicine* editors and I don't always agree, but I'm pleased to hear they share my view of how promising your work is."

I smiled and winked. "Promising enough that you might be interested in collaborating?"

Lowell laughed pleasantly. "You don't beat around the bush, do you? But the answer is yes, absolutely. The approaches both you and Carolyn have taken are ingenious and offer the kind of hope my patients so desperately need. I consider it my good fortune that Stan brought me to your attention as a substitute for Eric Salton."

I took a sip of coffee and nodded. "He was killed the night before I had a breakfast meeting set up with him. What an awful affair. I'm sure you knew him; were the two of you collaborators? Or friends?"

"No, we never worked together. And friends?" Lowell laughed again. But this time, it was a harsh guttural bark. "Not hardly. I hated his guts. If there was ever a man who needed killing, it was Eric Salton."

CHAPTER 13

I was flabbergasted. That was so inappropriate, so out of place, that I had no idea how to respond. Even though I remembered Karen saying the same thing after we heard Claire Weinstein's story.

Lowell saved me the trouble of trying to come up with a suitable reply. "I'm sorry. That was a crazy thing for me to say. It just came out. But I'm sure you've heard the stories about him. I guess you decided you'd be able to work with him anyway."

"Actually, I didn't hear about his history of sexual misconduct until after he was killed. I wouldn't have wanted him as a collaborator if I'd known, especially since the student working with me on this project is a young woman. But the forcefulness of your statement was striking. Did something happen between the two of you?"

He looked down at the table and nodded slowly. "Yes, I guess I owe you an explanation. An undergraduate who did an internship with me was one of his victims. She was a brilliant, sweet girl, and I became quite fond of her. Then she went to medical school in Boston and got a summer position with Salton. He started pressuring her for sex almost immediately, but she refused. That didn't stop him, and she had to become increasingly firm in her rejections. His response was to get her kicked out of school with some bullshit story about stealing drugs. She finally came to me for help, and I jumped in and demanded an emergency meeting with the dean." His voice broke, and he paused for a moment. "But it was too late," he continued. "She hanged herself before the meeting was even scheduled."

"Jesus! How terrible. I'm so sorry. I can understand how you feel."

He took a deep breath. "Thanks, Brad. I hope you won't hold my earlier outburst against me."

"Don't worry," I assured him. "My fiancée said the same thing after another young woman who turned him down told us what he did to her. That Salton was 'a man who needed killing.'" I glanced at my watch. "Are you okay to meet with Carolyn and the students, or do you need a few minutes? It's time for our little mini-symposium, and we should head down to the conference room if you're up to it."

He took a deep breath. "Sure, I'm ready."

I had a good feeling about Steve Lowell. But I was worried that what he'd said about Salton would eliminate any chance of a collaboration between us. I'd have to tell Karen, and I was sure she'd pass it on to Zelen. He'd need to expand his list of potential victims beyond clinical fellows to include younger women who'd worked with Salton. And he'd almost certainly consider the possibility that Lowell was the killer. Not by himself obviously, but he could have hired a woman to do the job.

I suspected Zelen would want to talk to him. And I didn't think that would leave Steve Lowell wanting to have anything further to do with me. I sighed inwardly. Maybe things would at least work out between him and Carolyn.

———

Carolyn and all three students were sitting at the conference room's twelve-seat table when we got there. I made the necessary introductions, and we all got sandwiches and drinks from a lunch selection I'd had brought in. There was a screen on the wall at the foot of the table for PowerPoint presentations, so I had Steve sit at the head while I took a seat on the side next to Ginger.

The plan was for Carolyn's students to present first, then Ginger, and finally to have an open discussion with Steve about how he thought we might proceed to clinical trials. Barbara Slotkin, the student of Carolyn's who'd done the initial AI work on drug discovery, was first up. I was a bit worried about how her talk would go, since I very much doubted that Steve had the computational background to understand the way the new tools of artificial intelligence could be used in drug development.

But I needn't have been concerned. Barbara gave a crystal-clear presentation, and it was obvious from the questions Steve asked that he was following closely. When she finished, he congratulated her and noted that her explanation of the use of AI in drug discovery was far better than the mumbo-jumbo he'd heard from some more senior scientists.

Penny Alberts, Carolyn's other student, then took over and presented her data on their drug's activity against both cancer cells in culture and tumors in mice. It was an impressive story. The drug was highly effective at killing cancer cells with abnormal *RAS* proteins but virtually inactive against normal cells. Just what one would want.

Steve didn't wait to respond enthusiastically. "This whole story is really impressive. I'd love to be involved in moving this to the clinic." Turning to me, he asked, "Should we talk now about how that might work or wait until Ginger presents her work?"

Carolyn responded before I had a chance. "Oh, let's wait until you hear Ginger's story. I think you'll be excited by that, too, and we can talk about the next stage for both projects together."

Steve agreed that sounded good, and Ginger got up to take her turn. As I expected, she gave an eloquent and thoroughly convincing presentation that left Steve shaking his head. "This is just great. These are two of the most exciting projects I've heard about in a long time, and I'd be thrilled to be involved with either one. But fortunately, I have the resources to work on both of them, if you give me the opportunity. Should we discuss how we could get clinical trials started?"

All three students nodded enthusiastically, and I invited Steve to take the lead.

"Okay, let me start with the basics," he began. "There are three phases of clinical trials required for FDA approval of a new drug. Phase one trials test whether the drug is safe to administer to people and how high a dose can be tolerated without severe side effects. They usually involve only a few dozen patients and are followed by phase two trials in which a larger number of patients, typically around a hundred, are treated with the drug to determine whether it works against their cancers. It saves time and has become increasingly common to combine phases one and two into a single phase one/two trial, which is what I'd like to do in your cases. Questions so far?"

Ginger raised her hand first. "I get the general idea, but could you tell us how a phase one/two trial would actually work?"

"Sure, good question. We'd start by testing five or six increasing doses of the drug for toxicity. A group of three people would get the lowest dose. If it's well tolerated, the next group would get a higher dose, and so forth. Once we establish the maximum tolerated dose, we'd expand the study by giving that dose to the full patient population to see whether it's effective against their cancers."

"And how would you determine that?" Ginger asked.

"We'd do scans at regular intervals to follow the tumors. Hopefully we'd see the tumors shrink or at least stop growing," Steve explained.

Barbara, Carolyn's computational student, was waving her

hand. "How do you really know how well the new drug is working, though? I mean, I know it's good if the tumors shrink, but
there are already lots of drugs available. How can you tell if the
new drug you're testing is any better than what's already out
there?"

Steve rewarded her with a smile. "Excellent point! Of course, we
know in a general way how well patients with the same type of
cancer respond to the treatments already in use, so we can get a
pretty good idea of how the new drug compares. But you're absolutely right. There's no control group in phase two trials, so we
can't draw any kind of rigorous scientific conclusion. Which is
where phase three comes in. I'll get to that next, but are there any
other questions first?"

There were none, and Steve continued. "Okay, if the phase two
results look good, we move on to phase three, in which the new
drug is directly compared to the current standard treatment. Phase
three trials involve a large number of patients, at least several
hundred, who are randomly divided into two groups. One group
receives the new drug while the other—the control group—receives
the best treatment currently in use. Now we can make a rigorous
comparison that tells us directly whether the new drug is better
than the best current treatment, which is what's needed for FDA
approval."

Barbara nodded her understanding. But Penny, Carolyn's other
student, looked troubled. Steve noticed and turned to her, asking if
she had a question.

"Not really a question. It's more of an ethical problem. We know
from all the experiments we've done in the lab that our drug works
better than what's available now. If you go on and confirm that it
works in phase two, it doesn't seem right to have a group of control
patients in phase three who get the current treatment instead. Do
they even know that's all they're going to get when they volunteer
for the trial?"

"I understand your concern," Steve replied. "And no, patients are assigned randomly to the new drug or control groups, so they don't know which treatment they're getting. But as Barbara pointed out, we don't really know whether the new drug is better without having a direct comparison to what's currently used. And that has to be done in clinical trials, because things just aren't always the same between mice and humans. There have been all too many drugs that looked great in the laboratory but flopped in the clinic."

Penny frowned and shook her head. "I understand what you're saying about lab results not translating to the clinic, but our new drug is more than twice as effective against a whole variety of cancer cell lines with mutant *RAS* genes than anything else that's available. It would be obvious from the phase two results whether it worked that well in patients. If it does, having a control group in phase three just means that half the patients who volunteered because they wanted the new drug won't get it. And some of them are going to get sicker or even die when they could have been helped."

Penny's face was flushed and sweaty. She was clearly agitated, and I was afraid this was going to go south. But Steve handled it well.

"I hear what you're saying. But the problem is that once a new drug is approved for general use, it'll be given to many, many people. Thousands of lives could be lost if it doesn't work as well as it should, so we have to be absolutely sure. That's why there's a strict requirement for a controlled comparison. But there are also established guidelines for stopping a trial early if patients receiving a new drug are doing significantly better than the controls. If that happens, the patients in the control group are offered the new drug as well. In a case as strong as the one you're positing, I can imagine the decision to stop a phase three trial might be made very early, before the control patients suffer any significant disadvantage. And who knows, perhaps someday the need for controls will be reevaluated. But we're not there yet, and we need to follow the accepted guidelines if we want our work to be meaningful. Does that make sense?"

Barbara and Ginger nodded agreement, but Penny just stared at the top of the table with her jaw clenched. I thought Steve's response had been highly appropriate and didn't need further discussion, so I decided to bring the session to a close.

I stood up and cleared my throat. "Perhaps we can talk more about this if our drugs do well enough to actually make it to phase three. For now, though, our guest is late for his next meeting, so we need to wrap this up. Steve, thank you for a very clear explanation of how clinical trials work." I initiated a round of applause and was joined by Carolyn and the students, including an obviously less-than-enthusiastic Penny.

Steve graciously responded by thanking the students for their presentations, and I started to take him down to Stan's office for the next meeting on his schedule.

As soon as we left the conference room, he asked about moving ahead with a collaboration. "I really would love to help with both of these projects. If you're agreeable, I'd be happy to draft protocols for phase one/two trials that we could then discuss in detail." He winked. "Either with or without the students."

I chuckled. "Might be easier without. But that sounds great. I'm sure Carolyn feels the same, and I'll let her know. And we'll both see you a bit later for your evening lecture."

He gave me a big grin. "Thank you so much again for arranging that. I really appreciate the opportunity to give a public lecture on the clinical aspects of drug development; it's something people should know about. Not to mention the chance to sell some copies of my new book afterward!"

CHAPTER 14

SHIRLEY

She wanted to sit near the front where she'd have a good view of his face, but the auditorium was almost full. Even though she was ten minutes early, the best she could do was a seat halfway to the back. *Doesn't matter*, she told herself, *this'll do*.

Promptly at six, Parker went to the podium and introduced the speaker. He made him sound like God's gift. Someone who helped people, even saved lives, by developing new cancer treatments. And not only that, Dr. Lowell didn't live in an ivory tower. He enjoyed explaining his work to the public in lectures like this, and he'd recently written a book on cancer for the general reader. Said book, Parker added, would be available at the reception following the lecture, which he hoped everyone would be able to attend. Then he asked the audience to welcome Dr. Lowell.

She had to admit he was a smooth speaker. He started off explaining the basics of drug development, beginning with the methods that could be used to identify new drugs, moving from there to laboratory testing, and finally to clinical trials. Then he talked about some of the drugs he'd worked on, not surprisingly focusing on the ones that had been successful and ignoring the many failures.

She lost focus as he droned on and on, making himself sound like a hero who was responsible for saving thousands of lives. Without any mention of the people he'd hurt along the way. He was an evil, shit-faced, disgusting liar. No better than Salton. And she knew what to do with men like that.

She could do it tonight. She had the knife with her, ready and waiting. She'd heard that he was going to spend the night at one of the motels on Wells Beach, so she could leave after the lecture was over and be waiting for him there after he sold his damn books at the reception. She could do it in the parking lot if nobody was around, or later in his room, or maybe even when he was taking an evening walk on the beach.

But that wouldn't be smart. There were too many tourists in Wells during the summer, too great a chance of being spotted. It would be better to wait for later, when he was back in Portland.

She left after the lecture with the rest of the audience, except she went out to her car instead of going to the reception. Then she removed the long black wig and cleaned off the makeup that gave her normally fair skin a swarthy complexion. A disguise that was not only effective, but also completely different from the one she'd used in Boston.

On the way home, she had the comforting thought that she could come up with as many different disguises as she needed.

CHAPTER 15

BRAD

Karen had come straight from her office and gotten to MTRI just before Lowell's lecture was about to start, so the first chance I had to talk to her was when we got home after the reception. It had been a long day, but I wanted to tell her about Lowell's visit, particularly what he'd had to say about Eric Salton.

In contrast to my reaction, she wasn't terribly surprised by his story. "Salton was a predatory monster. If he had younger students around him, he'd have seen them as just another pool of victims. It's disgusting, no question, but sadly not unexpected. I'll call Zelen in the morning; this'll give him another pool of potential victims to look into."

"What do you think about Lowell saying that Salton was 'a man who needed killing'?" I asked. "Might he have gone ahead and had it done?"

She shrugged. "I don't know, I remember saying the same thing after we talked to Claire Weinstein. Do you think I'm a suspect?"

I gave her a piercing look and pulled out my phone. "Hold on, I need to give Detective Zelen a call."

She laughed but then spoke seriously. "It's just an expression, and a perfectly reasonable way for him to feel. I don't think the relationship he had with the student would have made him kill for revenge. A lover might do that, but not a student's mentor."

"I'm glad to hear you say that. I liked him and was hoping we'd be able to work together. Do you think Zelen will want to talk to him?"

"Probably, but not as a suspect. He'll want to get the story himself, and he'll want to see if Lowell knows any other students who might have worked with Salton. But since Lowell couldn't have done it himself, it's not like he needs an alibi or that Zelen will want a DNA sample. I'll confirm with him tomorrow, but I'm sure he'll just have an informational chat with Lowell. Nothing intimidating that would sour a collaboration between the two of you."

"Good. I hope you're right about him not turning Lowell off."

She grinned. "Of course, I'm right. You know I'm always right."

"I do know that. My memory just fails sometimes."

We got a laugh out of one of our standing jokes before going up to bed.

———

She was, of course, right. I was signing off memos in my office the next day when Anna knocked on the door and said I had a call from Steve Lowell. I picked up the phone with some trepidation, which heightened when he began with, "Your Detective Zelen paid me a visit earlier today."

My Detective Zelen. I sighed, probably loudly enough to be heard over the phone. "I'm sorry. I hope he wasn't too much of a bother."

"No worries. It actually felt good to tell a cop what Salton had done to my student, even though it's too late for him to do anything about it. And Zelen seems like a nice guy. He went out of his way to explain that your fiancée was working with him on Salton's murder, so when you told her what had happened, she realized it was important and let him know. And he was very grateful for the information because it expanded the range of potential victims he was talking to."

I breathed easier. "I'm glad to hear it wasn't a problem. I was worried I'd set you up for an unpleasant police interrogation."

"Not at all. I even told him I hoped he didn't catch whoever did it. He laughed and said he could understand that; he was just doing his job."

I'd have to remember to thank Zelen for the velvet glove treatment. "Well, thanks for letting me know it went okay. I was a bit worried about how his talking with you would work out, so I appreciate your calling."

"That's only partly why I called, though," Steve said. "I've started working on protocols for phase one/two trials of the drugs we talked about. I hope you and Carolyn are still interested?"

"Absolutely! I'm ready to move full speed ahead, and I can assure you that Carolyn is too."

"Good. I've got the proposals pretty well drafted, but there are a few places where I could use some help."

"Sure. What do you need?" I asked.

"There are two major areas where I'd like guidance from you and Carolyn: the dose of drugs we should use and the criteria for patient eligibility. For your double-antibody ADC, I figure the dose should be in the same ballpark as other ADCs. Do you agree?"

"Sounds right to me. That's the kind of dose we used for our mouse experiments."

"Okay, that's easy then. How about patient eligibility? Do we want to restrict the study to patients whose tumors express some minimal level of the markers your ADC is targeting?"

I thought about that for a moment. Then I decided against. "No, I don't think so. We chose those markers because they're generally expressed on lung cancers, so let's make it open to all lung cancer patients."

"All right, that sounds good to me. And we'll have biopsies of all the patients' tumors, so we can always compare expression of the markers in patients that respond versus those that don't. That could give us valuable information for future studies."

"Good idea," I agreed. "Anything else about patient eligibility?"

"I can handle the rest. For an initial trial like this, eligible patients will have to have advanced disease that's failed to respond or relapsed after at least one standard therapy."

"Meaning their prognosis is poor enough that it makes sense for them to take a shot at an experimental treatment?" I asked.

"I'm afraid so. This is a shitty disease, despite all the years that folks like us have been working on it."

I sighed. "All too true. But we've made some progress over the years, and we've got to keep trying. In that regard, are you going to give Carolyn a call with similar questions?"

"I could, but I was actually thinking it might be useful for the three of us to meet and go over everything together. Since Carolyn's drug is targeted against a specific genetic change rather than a particular kind of cancer, patient selection is going to be more complicated and will take some discussion. And these study protocols wind up being pretty complex documents that I'd like to go over with the two of you before finalizing them. Any chance we could all get together for an hour or two?"

"Good idea, I'd like that. I'm sure Carolyn would too. How about I let her know, and assuming she's agreeable, we'll make the trip up to Portland this time."

"That'd be great," Steve said. "This is my month in clinic, so the end of the day would work best for me."

"No problem. I'll have my administrative assistant give you a call to coordinate schedules."

CHAPTER 16
SHIRLEY

She'd spent several days researching Lowell, including visiting Portland to check out his routine. Which was ridiculously simple. He got to his office early, left late, and went straight home. She could get him there, but he had a wife and kid, and they presented a complication she didn't want to deal with.

That left catching him in the hospital parking garage when he was either arriving in the morning or leaving at the end of the day. The problem was that it was a busy place, especially in the morning, so there was a high likelihood of being seen. But he usually didn't leave until six thirty or seven, and by then most of the other cars were gone.

That was the best choice, she decided. And she'd be properly disguised, so it wouldn't really matter if somebody saw her. Or if she got caught on a security camera in the garage.

Now that the day was here, she felt the same sense of excitement as when she'd gone to Boston to kill Salton. The thrill of a hunt that would soon bring justice that had been too long delayed.

She parked two blocks away, walked to the hospital, and went in through the main entrance. Then she took the stairs down to the garage, located Lowell's car, and found a dark corner with a view of the stairwell. Satisfied with the setup, she put on a plastic poncho that would protect her from blood spatter and settled in to wait.

The garage was two-thirds empty and nobody else was around when Lowell emerged from the stairwell. *Perfect.* But then she saw there were two other people with him, and her jaw dropped. *Parker and Gelman! What the hell was going on?*

Astonishment turned to fear when they started walking in her direction, rather than toward Lowell's car. Should she run or pretend she was innocently waiting for someone else? She was confident of her disguise, but a stranger loitering in the garage would be more than a little suspicious. What if they called security?

But they stopped at another car well before they got to her. Gelman got in the passenger side, and Parker got behind the wheel after a final exchange with Lowell. She couldn't hear what they were saying, but their smiles and back-slapping clearly signified the conclusion of a successful meeting.

She finally breathed easier when Parker drove off and Lowell started over to his own car. Now was the time.

"Dr. Lowell," she called out.

He turned toward her with a surprised look. "Yes? Can I help you?"

She didn't say anything. Just kept walking toward him, with the poncho's hood over her head. And her knife in her hand.

"Do I know you?" he asked. And then he saw the knife.

His eyes widened and his mouth opened to scream, but she plunged the knife into his chest before the sound came out. He managed to grab her arm in a last-ditch attempt to fight for his life, but it was too late. She could see the strength leave his body as the blood spurted from the wound and he sank to the ground.

She slit his throat as he lay there. Just to be sure. And because she enjoyed it.

Then she reached into his back pocket and found a wallet. She removed the cash and tossed the empty wallet a few yards from his body. With a little luck, the stupid cops would think he'd been killed during a mugging.

After a careful check to be sure nothing was left behind, she went back to her dark corner and took off her gloves and poncho, which were now covered with his blood. Then she took out a mirror and made sure there was no other blood on her. Once she was satisfied, she put everything back into her tote bag with the knife, walked across the parking garage to the stairwell, and left the hospital through the main entrance, the same way she'd come in.

When she was back in her car, she removed her wig and used a wet nap to clean off her makeup. Then she drove home, stopping at a dumpster along the way to dispose of the poncho, gloves, and wig.

But she kept her knife. She wasn't finished yet.

CHAPTER 17

BRAD

Carolyn and I spent the trip home exulting in our meeting with Steve. He was amazingly thorough and detail-oriented, while at the same time being fun to work with. By the end of an intense ninety minutes, the three of us had everything planned out, the trial protocols were drafted, and we were excited about moving forward.

Carolyn had left her car at MTRI, so I dropped her off there before heading home myself, eager to tell Karen how well the day had gone. I was thinking it called for a celebratory dinner at Hobbs, our favorite restaurant, when the phone chimed with Karen's special ringtone.

I picked it up with a smile. "Hi there, I'm just on my way home from MTRI. Don't suppose I could talk you into a little lobster feast at Hobbs, could I?"

"Brad, hold on. I have to tell you something. If you're driving, you better pull off the road."

My stomach sank. This sounded bad. I pulled over and forced myself to speak calmly. "All right, go ahead. What's wrong?"

"I'm in Portland. At a murder scene."

That was unfortunate, but emergencies came with her job. We could celebrate another night. "Oh, so you won't be—"

"Brad, let me finish! The victim is Steve Lowell."

I felt faint, like someone had pumped the air out of the car and started it spinning on one of its back wheels. This wasn't real. It couldn't be!

I realized I hadn't said anything when I heard Karen's anxious voice through the phone. "Brad, are you there? Are you okay?"

"That can't be," I managed to get out. "We were with him less than an hour ago."

"I know, you texted when you were leaving. That's when he was killed, in the parking garage. Brad, I'm so sorry!"

I took a moment to breathe deeply and get myself back under control. "What happened? He went down to the garage with Carolyn and me, and he was fine when we left him."

"He was knifed. They took the money out of his wallet, so it was probably a mugging. Did you see anybody else in the garage?"

"There was somebody I noticed standing in a corner, but I didn't really get a look them. Do you think that could have been the killer?"

"It's possible," Karen said. "I hate to ask this, but if you're okay to drive, can you come back up here? The detectives are going to need to talk to you."

"And they'll want to do it sooner rather than later," I added from experience. "Yeah, I can come back now."

———

The street in front of the parking garage was filled with cop cars when I got there. Some Portland police cruisers, some state patrol cars, a medical examiner van, and several cars that were unmarked, including Karen's. I parked behind her Volvo and walked up to the garage entrance, which was sealed off with crime scene tape. I spotted Karen in the middle of the garage and ducked under the tape to go to her. Only to be stopped by a burly state trooper.

"Where the hell do you think you're going, bud? Can't you tell this is a crime scene?"

It would be nice at times like this to have a badge I could flash. But I didn't, so I had to explain myself. "Sorry, Officer. I didn't see you. I'm Dr. Brad Parker. Lieutenant Richmond asked me to meet her here."

"She did, huh? You think I'm an idiot? You're probably a goddamn reporter. Get out of here, before I toss your ass in a cell."

I really wasn't in the mood for this, so rather than answering, I yelled out to Karen as loudly as I could. She turned just as the cop grabbed my arm.

"Let him through!" she shouted.

The cop's jaw dropped. "Ma'am? You know this creep?"

Karen apparently wasn't in the mood for nonsense either. "Are you stupid or what?" she yelled. "I said, let him through. He's our only witness, who also happens to be my fiancé."

This time the trooper turned pale and released my arm. "Yes, ma'am. I'm sorry ma'am, I didn't know." Holding up the tape for me, he added, "Please, sir, right this way. I'm so sorry, sir."

"Stop groveling, she's not going to fire you," I muttered as I ducked under the tape and went over to Karen.

When I reached her, she asked, "What'd you say to that jerk? He looks like he's in shock."

I shrugged. "Just told him to stop groveling. You weren't going to fire him."

She rolled her eyes. "Maybe I should. Oh well, let's get to work. Brad, this is Sergeant Randall. He'll be primary on the case, so he'll take your testimony, okay?"

I said that was fine, and Randall took over. "I understand you had a meeting with the victim shortly before he was killed. What was that about?"

"I'm working—was working—with him on clinical trials that

we were planning to run. I was here together with one of my colleagues, Carolyn Gelman, to finish drafting the protocols for those trials."

"Carolyn Gelman was at the meeting with you and the victim?"

"Correct. We drove up here from Wells together," I added.

Randall nodded. "What time did you get here?"

"We were planning to meet at five, right after Steve finished in the clinic for the day. I think we got here a few minutes late, because he was waiting for us in his office."

"Was he alone, or was someone else involved in the meeting from his side?" Randall asked.

"No. It was just Steve, Carolyn, and me. We worked on the protocols for around an hour and a half, and then we all came down here together."

"Do you recall what time that was?"

"Steve emailed us copies of the finished protocols just before we left his office, so let me check my phone, and I can give you the exact time." I took a quick look. "The email came in at six thirty-two."

"And you would have gotten down here when? Five minutes or so after that?"

"Probably less. We just walked down a stairwell that wasn't far from his office."

"Okay, let's say about six thirty-five. Did you see anybody on the way down? Or here in the garage?"

"Not on the way down, but I did get a glimpse of someone standing in the corner over there."

I pointed to the corner across from us, and Randall nodded. "Got it. Can you describe them?"

"Sorry, no. They were behind a pillar, and all I could see was somebody in a dark-blue hooded coat or poncho of some sort."

Randall took out his phone. "Is this the person you saw?"

The image was a blurry shot of someone whose face was obscured by a hood. I shrugged. "Maybe. It looks like the kind of poncho I remember, but beyond that I can't say. Is this from security video?"

"Yeah. And unfortunately, it's all we have. But it was taken at six thirty-eight, which fits your timeline and makes whoever it is a prime suspect. Did you see anything else when the three of you got down here?"

"Nothing. Steve walked Carolyn and me over to my car, we got in, and I pulled out. He'd just started to walk away, presumably to his car, when we left."

"And just to be clear, you and Gelman drove back to Wells together?" Randall asked.

"Correct. Karen mentioned earlier that it looked like he was mugged. Is that still what you're thinking?"

"It's our best guess," Randall confirmed. "The body was found around seven by another doctor. It was near the victim's car, and his wallet, minus any cash, was on the ground nearby. The victim had been stabbed in the chest and his throat slashed. Putting what we have together, it suggests that blue poncho was waiting down here hoping to spot an easy mark. Once you left, our victim was alone and fit the bill. Unfortunately, he probably made the mistake of trying to put up a fight instead of just giving up his money."

I shook my head sadly. "Seems like he would've been smarter than that, but I guess you can never tell what people are going to do in that kind of situation. Did you find any of the assailant's prints or DNA?"

"Afraid not," Randall said. "The wallet was clean, so the mugger probably wore gloves and was careful not to leave evidence behind. We'll talk to Carolyn Gelman, just in case she noticed something you didn't. But failing that, this is the kind of senseless killing that never gets solved."

CHAPTER 18

I was too upset by Steve Lowell's death to even start thinking about alternative approaches to getting our clinical trials started. I knew it was ridiculous, but I couldn't shake the feeling that I was somehow responsible. And ridiculous or not, the fact remained that I'd approached two clinicians as collaborators—Eric Salton and Steve Lowell—both of whom had been murdered. The odds of that happening by chance had to be vanishingly small. If I believed in such things, I'd think that my recruiting someone else would be the kiss of death. But, of course, I wasn't superstitious. . . .

Karen finally broke through my funk when we were walking Rosie on the beach one evening after dinner. "You want to tell me what's going on? You've been strangely withdrawn ever since Steve Lowell was killed. Are you blaming yourself because the situation was so similar to Salton's case?"

I nodded glumly. "I know it's ridiculous. But yes, I'm afraid that's exactly what I'm doing."

"I'm not surprised. In some ways, it's natural for you to react like that. But as much as I love you, you know you're only human, right? Not some mythical demon who brings death to anyone who considers collaborating with him."

I couldn't help laughing at that. "Yeah, I guess you're right."

"Good, that sounds like progress. So have you come up with any ideas for who you can work with instead of Lowell?"

"I suspect you know the answer to that. I haven't even been able to make myself think about it."

"Well, start thinking about it then. You owe it to Carolyn to get things back on track. And for that matter, to your student who's done the work with you. Not to mention the cancer victims who might be helped by the new treatments."

That put things in a different perspective. Letting myself be paralyzed by guilt about Steve was a selfish indulgence that was unfair to my colleagues. And perhaps even more unfair to unknown patients who desperately needed help. It was time to get back to work.

I reached over and squeezed her shoulder. "You're right. I'll talk to Stan and Carolyn tomorrow and start figuring out how to proceed."

"Good. And now, how about going back inside where it's a bit more private? I have some thoughts on how to keep you from brooding about Steve Lowell for a while."

———

I went to see Carolyn as soon as I got to MTRI the next morning. As usual, most of the floor space in her office was occupied by Molly, her 125-pound Newfoundland. Karen and I had rescued Molly after her owner had been shot, and rather than taking her to a shelter, we'd brought her to MTRI to meet Carolyn. It had been love at first sight, and Molly had a new human and a new home. She was always excited to see me, no doubt grateful because I'd hooked her up with Carolyn, so the first thing I did was get down on the floor for our usual cuddling session.

When I got up, Carolyn was smiling at me from behind her desk. "Haven't seen you for a while, Brad. Didn't think you could stay away from Molly for so long."

"I'm sorry—" I started to say, but she cut me off.

"I know, Steve Lowell's murder got to you. To me too, but I think you were quite a bit closer to him than I was."

"Yeah, he and I really clicked. I couldn't deal with figuring out another approach to our clinical trials. But now I'm ready."

"Good, I'm glad to have you back. So, what're you thinking?"

"Nothing beyond talking to Stan," I admitted. "That's how we got started with Steve. Hopefully, he'll have another idea."

"I may have gotten ahead of you on that," Carolyn said. "Stan came to see me two days after Steve was killed. He'd just heard about it, and I guess you weren't around."

I nodded, remembering. "I had to go to a trustees' meeting that afternoon."

She rolled her eyes. "That was fun, I'm sure. Anyway, after we chatted for a bit, he asked whether our collaboration with Steve had gotten started. When I told him we'd gotten as far as drafting protocols, he asked to see them, so I sent him the versions Steve had sent us."

I was intrigued. "What'd he think?"

"Wait a sec, I'll show you his email. It may solve our problem."

She fiddled with her computer and then turned it toward me so I could see the screen.

Carolyn,

These protocols look great. As I expected, Steve did a terrific job. Unfortunately, now that he's gone, I don't have any ideas for finding another outside collaborator.

Maybe at this point we should think about moving forward on our own. The way Steve set it up, the phase I/II trials for both you and Brad are small enough that we could manage them here if you'd be willing to take on the role of medical director. I can help with some of the work, but I'm already overcommitted and would need you to take the lead.

Let me know what you think. If you're game, doing it ourselves might be the simplest way to go.

Stan

It was an interesting idea, and I certainly liked the option of not trying to find a replacement for Steve. But it would be a substantial burden on Carolyn, and I didn't want to push her into it.

I kept my response noncommittal. "I don't know. Doing it here would undoubtedly be easier in some ways, but it would mean a big commitment from you. I can help and provide administrative support, but since I'm not an MD, there's only so much I can do. I'm sure Stan would pitch in, but I'm afraid most of the work would fall on your shoulders."

"True. But being able to combine clinical and basic research is the reason I got both MD and PhD degrees in the first place. And directing two fairly small trials like this wouldn't be that bad. Or have you forgotten that I've run a clinical trial before?"

No way I could forget that. When I'd first come to MTRI as interim director, Carolyn had a trial in progress. Unfortunately, someone was making a major effort to sabotage her work. When they went so far as poisoning two of Carolyn's patients, Karen—who was then with the FBI—became involved. It eventually turned out that the culprit was another faculty member at MTRI who had fabricated data to obtain FDA approval of a drug of his own, and Carolyn's results were on the verge of exposing his fraud. In the end, he'd been properly dealt with, but it had been hard going and certainly nothing that any of us would ever forget.

"Oh, I remember that all too well," I said. "And this one would presumably be far less traumatic. But it would place major demands on what we both know is your already full schedule. Bottom line, it's a great idea from my standpoint, but you're the one who'd have to do the bulk of the work. So it's really up to you."

"Good. At this point, I think it'll be easier for me to just step up and do it than it would be to try to find someone else from outside.

Let's get together with Stan, and we'll get moving. Should we have a joint meeting with our lab people to tell them about the change in plans?"

"Sounds good to me. I'll email Stan and see if he can meet with us this afternoon. And I'll ask Anna to set up a joint lab meeting sometime in the next couple of days."

She grinned and winked at me. "Great, thanks. I think I'm going to like having you as my new administrative assistant."

CHAPTER 19

'd just finished meeting with Carolyn and Stan to map out the start of our trials when my phone buzzed. When I saw it was a text from Karen, I started mentally drafting a message thanking her for the nudge and telling her that we'd gotten the trials back on track. Then I looked at what she'd written.

On the run to hostage situation in Kittery, no time to explain. But big breakthrough. Meeting Zelen to strategize, Capital Grille in Burlington at seven. Join us. Fill you in then.

I stared at my phone. It must be a breakthrough in the Salton case if she was rushing to confer with Zelen. But it was his case, not Karen's, so what the hell could it be? I took a deep breath. It sounded like I'd have to wait for the answer, so I simply texted back, *Okay* and started home to take care of Rosie. There was just time to feed and walk her before I'd have to leave for the restaurant.

The Capital Grille was a nationwide chain of high-end steak-houses that were reliably good. When I'd first moved to Maine, and Karen was still in Boston, we met for dinner regularly at the one in Burlington, a small town northwest of Boston. Meeting there made for a significantly shorter trip from Maine than going all the way into the city, which I assumed was why she'd suggested it to Zelen.

I spotted Karen's car in the parking lot when I got to the restaurant and then saw that she was still in it talking on the phone. She didn't notice me until I tapped on the window, at which she smiled and mouthed, "One minute." When she finished, she got out and gave me a kiss. "This has been one helluva day! But Zelen texted a few minutes ago, saying that he's already here. Let's go find him, and I'll tell both of you what's happened."

I was surprised at that. "Zelen doesn't know either?"

"No, I just told him what I told you. Sorry, it was too crazy for me to have time for explanations. Guy shot his wife, kidnapped their two kids, and was holed up in his house with them as hostages."

"Jesus. It got resolved okay?"

She rolled her eyes. "How could something like that be okay? The negotiator couldn't talk him down, and the SWAT guys eventually had to shoot him. But he's in the hospital and will be all right. Kids are fine physically. Emotionally, all we can do is hope for the best. I doubt if 'okay' will ever apply."

There wasn't much I could say to that, so I just squeezed her hand as we entered the restaurant. Karen spotted Zelen sitting at a well-appointed bar on our right, nursing what looked like an oversized martini. We went over to him, and Karen suggested we get a table so we could talk.

As soon as we were seated in the elegant mahogany-paneled dining room, a waiter materialized to take our drink orders. I asked for a single malt scotch, Karen ordered a glass of sauvignon blanc, and Zelen said he'd just nurse the remains of his martini and have a glass of wine with dinner. Then Karen suggested that we go ahead and order, since the main choice was simply what variety of steak we wanted. It only took a glance at the menu for Karen and me to decide on filet mignons and Zelen on a bone-in ribeye. We added sides of grilled asparagus and au gratin potatoes for the table and a bottle of pinot noir to be served with our dinners.

When the waiter left, Zelen raised the question. "Okay, how about finally telling me what we're here for?"

Karen smiled. "Yep, now's the time. I'm sure Brad's dying to know too."

Zelen shot me a questioning look, and I shook my head. "No, she hasn't told me either." Then we both turned our full attention to Karen.

"You remember Steve Lowell?" she asked Zelen.

"Sure. He's the one who told Brad about the undergraduate that Salton harassed."

"Right. But what you probably don't know is that he was murdered a week ago. And my surprise news is that Lowell and Salton were both killed by the same woman."

Zelen's mouth flopped open, registering the same surprise that struck me.

When I was able to speak, I said, "Wait a minute. I thought whoever killed Lowell was careful not to leave any DNA or prints. Did you catch them on a video somewhere?"

Karen shook her head. "The medical examiner found a bit of skin under Lowell's fingernails. He must have tried to put up a fight and scratched his killer. Anyway, the ME got DNA from that, and it matched the crime scene DNA from Salton's killer that's in CODIS."

"So the same woman killed them both." I spoke slowly, still trying to digest this new development. "But you don't know who it is."

Zelen shook his head and held up his glass to signal the waiter for another drink. Then he turned to Karen. "I think you better tell me what the hell's going on. And I'm pretty sure I'm gonna need another martini to make sense of this story."

CHAPTER 20

By the time Karen filled Zelen in, he'd downed half of his second martini, and our dinners had been served. When the waiter left us, Zelen took another gulp and turned to me. "Okay, I've got the crime scene and ME perspectives. Brad, tell me more about Lowell. What were you meeting with him about before he was killed?"

"It was strictly science. He'd agreed to collaborate with Carolyn Gelman and me in running clinical trials and had put together a draft version of protocols. The three of us met to review his draft and go over some of the final details."

"Anything come up that might be related to his murder?" Zelen asked.

I shook my head firmly. "No, nothing. My first meeting with him, when he visited MTRI, was the one that was revealing."

"That was when he told you about the student who'd worked with him and then become one of Salton's victims?"

"Right. And how much he hated Salton."

Zelen nodded and drank some more of his martini. It would be gone soon, and I wondered if he'd have a third or switch to wine.

He seemed to be lost in thought, so I had some steak and tried the asparagus while I waited for his next question. Karen, of course, had been chowing down steadily, and she had just enough steak left to take a treat home to Rosie.

When he looked up again, Zelen offered his summary of the situation. "Seems to me that the unfortunate student Salton harassed is the only link we have between him and Lowell. Connie Hillyard was her name, by the way."

"I think that's right," I agreed. "But it's not much of a link. Lowell was her mentor and tried to help her, while Salton harassed her and had her thrown out of school, which drove her to suicide."

Karen glanced at Zelen, and I could feel something pass between them. Then she put a hand on my arm. "I know you liked Lowell, and that's how he told the story. But there might be more to his relationship with Connie. What if he went beyond being her mentor and became her lover?"

"That would be consistent with how furious he was at Salton," Zelen added.

If both Karen and Zelen thought that was credible, I had to consider it. But it was so at odds with my own take on Lowell that I didn't buy it.

"I can't see it. In fact, I don't think the idea that Lowell had an inappropriate relationship with Connie fits his reaction to Salton at all. He was blatantly disgusted with Salton for wanting to have sex with her. That's not the way he'd have felt if he'd had sex with her himself."

"I wouldn't be so sure of that," Karen countered. "If Lowell did have a relationship with Connie, it was presumably caring and consensual. Nothing like Salton's harassment."

"Exactly," Zelen seconded. "Which would have made him all the more angry at Salton."

I held up my hands in a gesture of surrender. "All right, I get what you guys are saying. But even if you're right, what difference does it make at this point? Connie obviously didn't kill either one of them."

"No, but we need to consider the possibility that somebody close to Connie killed them both to avenge her death," Karen said. "A relative, a romantic partner, a close friend. In fact, that could have happened even if Lowell's relationship with her was completely above board. Someone stricken by Connie's death might have killed Lowell because they *thought* he'd taken advantage of her, even if he hadn't."

"That sounds more plausible," I conceded. "He was certainly fond of her, and that could have been misconstrued. Do we know anything about Connie's family or friends?"

Zelen consulted his notebook. "I got some information from her medical school file. Her only living relative was her mother, who lives in Lexington. I talked to her last week, and as you might expect, she hated Salton. But she was on a trip to New York the night he was killed, and the two friends she was with vouched for her alibi. I'll go back, though, and see what she thought about Connie's relationship with Lowell, as well as what she can tell us about Connie's friends. But Karen, thinking of these as related revenge killings suggests another possibility."

"I agree." Karen picked up his line of thought. "Connie might not be the only student who crossed paths with both Lowell and Salton. I assume you can send me a list of Salton's former students and fellows?"

Zelen nodded, and she continued. "Okay. I'll put together a list of Lowell's for comparison. And I'll also interview Lowell's associates to see if there's been any talk of his getting involved with students. Does that cover it?"

"I think so. Let's hope this takes us somewhere." Zelen drained his martini. "I sure as hell haven't gotten anywhere just looking at women who were clinical fellows with Salton. Even the two I thought were good candidates because they left oncology turned out to be duds."

CHAPTER 21

Karen left early the next morning to go to Portland with two of her detectives. She was planning to collect information on Lowell's former students and fellows to compare with the list of Salton's that Zelen had sent her. In the meantime, the detectives would question Lowell's colleagues to explore any possibility of sexual misconduct. She and Zelen had already set a time to talk this evening and compare notes.

I was highly skeptical about Lowell having engaged in anything inappropriate, but the possibility of additional overlaps between his students and Salton's could prove interesting. As could whatever Zelen learned from talking to Connie's mother and possibly to other friends and relatives. So I was looking forward to this evening's debriefing.

But first, this afternoon was the meeting that Anna had arranged for Carolyn and me to update our students on the clinical trial status. Carolyn still hadn't arrived when I got to the conference room, but the others were waiting around the table, so I distributed copies of the protocols and got started.

"I'm sure Carolyn will be here soon, and she won't mind if we get going. As I think you all know, we were planning to collaborate with Steve Lowell on clinical trials of the drugs you guys have been working on. He was very excited about both projects, and we got off to a great start on planning the trials together. Then, everything came to a halt when he was tragically killed."

"My God! What happened?" Barbara, Carolyn's computational student, gasped.

"He was knifed by a mugger," Carolyn responded, having just entered the room. "Right after Brad and I finished a meeting with him."

"How awful!" Ginger cried, as Carolyn's second student—Penny—shook her head and muttered, "Terrible."

"Have the police found whoever killed him?" Ginger asked.

"They're still investigating," I said. "But what we want to talk to you about is how we're planning to move forward without him."

Penny raised her hand. "Have you found another clinical person to work with already?"

Carolyn responded before I had a chance to say anything. "No, we've decided to do it ourselves, here at the institute. Brad and I met with Steve before he was killed to finalize protocols for the initial trials, which I see Brad has already passed around. I showed them to Stan Jacobs, the institute's clinical director, to get his opinion. He was impressed with how straightforward they were and thought, since all of this preliminary work was already done, we should go ahead and run the trials here in our own clinic."

"That's dependent, of course, on Carolyn being willing to step into the clinical trial director role," I added. "I can help to some extent, but since I'm not an MD, what I can do is pretty limited. That leaves Carolyn with a lot of additional responsibility, and I have to say I'm really grateful to her for taking it on."

I started a small round of applause, to which Carolyn laughed and held up a hand. "All right guys, thanks. But it won't be that big a deal. The numbers of patients in both trials are fairly small, and I've run clinical trials before. Why don't you take a look at the protocols Brad passed around? Then we can talk through them and see if you have any questions or suggestions."

Carolyn gave them a few minutes and then continued. "So we're going to do combined phase one/two trials for both drugs. As Steve discussed with you, the initial phase will pinpoint a dose that doesn't cause serious toxicity, and we'll then use that dose in the second phase to determine its activity against tumors. Hopefully to see that it causes tumor regression or at least stops further growth. We'll aim to enroll around fifty lung cancer patients in each trial. For Brad and Ginger's double-antibody ADC, all lung cancer patients will be eligible. For my lab's anti-*RAS* drug, we'll screen biopsies of the tumors for the specific *RAS* mutation the drug targets and only enroll those patients we expect to be sensitive."

Ginger interrupted. "Will it be hard to find patients with the mutation?"

"I don't think it'll be too difficult," Carolyn answered. "About ten percent of lung cancers have the *RAS* mutation we want, and lung cancer is terribly common. We see more than a thousand cases each year here in Maine. And again, we're keeping the number of patients on the small side."

"How long will these trials go on?" Barbara asked.

"Depends on the results. If things look promising, a year or longer. But if the drugs aren't well tolerated or simply don't work, the trials would be terminated early."

"How will you decide whether the drugs 'work'?" Barbara continued. "I know I asked Dr. Lowell the same question, but if you don't have an untreated control group, there's nothing you can compare the treated patients to."

"That's only partially true," Carolyn replied. "To be eligible for either of these trials, a patient would have to have advanced cancer that's failed to respond to at least one type of standard treatment. We know that those patients have only about a twenty percent chance of responding, even transiently, to the conventional second-line treatments. So we'd be pretty happy if, say, half the patients responded to our experimental anti-*RAS* drug."

"And for our double-antibody ADC, we have even more direct data to compare it with," Ginger chimed in. "Around thirty to forty percent of patients respond to the single-antibody versions, so we can see if the double does better."

Barbara shook her head and addressed Carolyn. "You'd never let me design a mouse experiment like that. You'd say it was really sloppy science not to have controls."

Carolyn laughed. "You're right, that's exactly what I'd say. But people aren't mice. These patients are volunteering because they know the other options available to them aren't very good and they're hoping our new drug will work. In these early phases, we give them the best shot we can. But if the phase two results look good, the drug would move on to phase three. That would be a much larger trial and would have to include a control group of patients who receive the best available standard treatment for comparison."

"That part of it's just not right," Penny blurted out. "Like you said, these poor people have a terrible disease and are volunteering for an experimental drug because none of the available treatments are very good. But you're going to make half of them get the standard treatment as controls, even when you already know from phase two that the new drug is better. They're going to get a crappy treatment, just so that it's more rigorous science. I'm sorry, I think that sucks!"

This was the same meltdown she'd had when Steve explained how phase III trials work, and I decided to step in so that Carolyn wouldn't have to bear the brunt of arguing with her own student. Maybe I'd have better luck getting her to understand.

"But Penny, we don't know whether the new drug is better, not definitively, from just phase two results. It might be promising, like the example Carolyn gave, but the number of patients is small and, as Barbara pointed out, there's nothing to directly compare the results to. Having a randomized control group is the only way to know for sure. And as Steve explained, if the new drug turns out to be doing better than the standard treatment in phase three, the trial would be stopped early, and the patients in the control group would be switched to the experimental drug."

Penny's lower lip trembled. "But their cancers would be worse by then. Even if you can't always tell how good a new drug is from the phase two results, sometimes I think you should be able to. And for those drugs, having control groups in phase three isn't right."

I started to respond, but Carolyn put a restraining hand on my arm. "Let it go," she whispered. "I'll try to talk to her more about this later."

I let Carolyn give a nonconfrontational response and conclude the meeting. For some reason, the issue of a control patient group triggered a highly emotional reaction from Penny. I could understand her point of view, but her vehemence made me wonder if the thought of patients not getting the best possible treatment resonated with something from her past.

CHAPTER 22

Karen had texted that she was running late and would make it home just in time for our videoconference with Zelen at seven. That left me to come up with something for dinner that would be quick and flexible. I was thinking of picking up subs, but then I remembered that we had French onion soup in the freezer. I'd put together a good recipe a few months ago, and it had become one our favorite dinners. It took a while to prepare but it could be frozen, so I always made a double batch, which was convenient for nights like this when we wanted something quick.

Once I got home, I defrosted the soup in the microwave, toasted rounds of a French baguette for croutons, and sliced plenty of Gruyère cheese. All that remained was to heat the soup in oven-proof crocks, top it with the croutons and Gruyère, and stick it under the broiler for two or three minutes whenever we were ready for it.

As it turned out, Karen came through the front door about twenty minutes before seven, so we had time for a quick dinner before connecting with Zelen. Then we set up my laptop on the living room coffee table, sat next to each other on the couch, and hit the Zoom link.

When we had established the connection, Zelen asked Karen how her trip to Portland had gone.

"Kind of mixed," she reported. "I had two detectives spend the day trying to dig up dirt on Lowell. They came up with zilch. Most of his colleagues thought he was a saint, and those who didn't just had professional jealousy gripes."

"So nothing like Salton's rotten reputation?" Zelen asked.

"Not a bit. But I had more luck looking for trainees that he and Salton had in common. There were two women who were residents with Lowell and then went on to work with Salton, Edelle Schwartz and Francine Darcy. Did you talk to either of them when you canvassed Salton's clinical fellows?"

Zelen took a moment to consult a notebook. "As a matter of fact, I interviewed both of them. They're both at Harvard-affiliated hospitals and seem to have successful careers. Schwartz said she'd heard rumors about Salton harassing some of the women who worked with him, but he never bothered her. Darcy said he'd approached her, but she turned him down, and that was the end of it. Just to be thorough, I asked them both for DNA samples, which ruled them out."

Karen sighed. "Well, so much for my day in Portland. How about you? Any luck looking for people connected to Connie Hillyard?"

"I'm hoping," Zelen said. "I talked to her mother again. Turns out that she had mixed feelings about Lowell. She said Connie spoke very fondly of him, and they spent lots of time together when she was working with him. Including evenings and weekends. She thought it was strange that an older man would be so interested in her daughter, and she pressed Connie several times for signs that anything inappropriate was going on. But, according to Connie, it was all work and completely above board. Nonetheless, Mom said she was never completely satisfied. Even if nothing had happened, she never stopped wondering if Lowell had been grooming her daughter."

This was starting to sound like we might have a plausible suspect. Except Zelen had said she was on a trip to New York the night of Salton's murder. Still, a New York to Boston round trip would only take a few hours. I cleared my throat. "I know last night you said she was in New York when Salton was killed, but is there any chance she made a quick trip back to Boston in the middle of her New York visit?"

Zelen nodded. "Good question. She went to New York with two friends, whom I talked to after my first visit with her. They both said that the three of them were together the entire time, so her alibi seemed solid. Nonetheless, I asked her for a DNA sample, and that verified she's not the killer. But she also told me that Connie's closest friend since high school, Leslie Berk, was convinced that Connie and Lowell were having sex. And Leslie was hysterical with rage against Lowell as well as Salton after Connie's death."

Karen rolled her eyes. "Why the hell didn't she mention Leslie the first time you talked to her?"

Zelen gave an exaggerated shrug. "She said she didn't think it was important and didn't want to cause Leslie any trouble. But when I started asking about Connie and Lowell, she had second thoughts."

"Don't you love it when people decide what we need to know and what we don't?" Karen remarked. "Oh well, at least she finally came through. And Leslie sounds like somebody we should talk to. Have you been able to locate her?"

"Mm-hmm. Connie's mother told me that she's a molecular biologist. Up in your neck of the woods, at Jackson Laboratory."

"How convenient. Should we pay her a joint visit?" Karen suggested. "It's a long drive from Boston, so you might want to make it an overnight."

Zelen shook his head. "I've got a triple homicide pressing and won't be able to get away for that long until next week. Could you go ahead and talk to her without me?"

"Sure. And she sounds like a strong enough suspect that we should keep this moving. I'll go up there tomorrow."

"With a DNA analyzer so you can make an arrest?" Zelen asked.

Karen raised an eyebrow and gave him a wry smile. "Gee, I never would have thought of that."

After we disconnected, I asked Karen if she wanted me to come with her. I didn't doubt she could handle it herself, but it wouldn't hurt for me to go along.

"Up to you," she said. "If I remember correctly, it's nearly a four-hour drive from here to Bar Harbor, so some company would be nice if you're free."

CHAPTER 23

I searched the Jackson Lab website for Leslie Berk while Karen drove us up to Bar Harbor. She was a postdoctoral fellow working on the molecular biology of aging with Dr. Bill Arnold, whose lab was on the third floor of the North Research Building. That was a start to locating her, but since the Jackson Laboratory included sixty-eight buildings spread over more than a hundred and fifty acres, it took a while to find the right place. When we got there, two state troopers were waiting for us as backup, as Karen had requested.

The troopers stayed in the lobby while Karen and I went up to the third floor to interview the suspect. However, there were only three people in the Arnold lab when we got there. All men.

Karen muttered, "Shit, do you think she's not here today?" while I went over and asked the nearest one if he knew where we could find Leslie Berk. When he said she was across the hall in the microscope room, I breathed a sigh of relief.

The microscope room was dark and small, not much more than a hundred square feet, with a table holding three scopes on one of the side walls. A young woman with butch-cut black hair was using a fluorescence microscope at the front of the room. She glared at us and asked, "Who the hell are you? Salespeople? Can't you see I'm busy."

In response, Karen held up her badge. "Police. Are you Leslie Berk?"

She sighed resignedly. "Yeah, that's me. What's this about?"

"We have a few questions. Is there someplace we can talk? It's about Connie Hillyard."

She furrowed her brow. "Right here is fine." Indicating the lab stools in front of the other two microscopes, she added, "You can sit on those."

We squeezed around her and sat down. Then Karen asked how long she'd known Connie.

"Ever since high school. But we can skip the preliminaries. I assume you're here to ask me about her relationships with Eric Salton and Steve Lowell."

That took me by surprise. I glanced over at Karen and saw her eyes widen, even though I could tell she was trying to maintain a cop's poker face.

"Why would you assume that?" she asked.

"Connie's mother called last night to tell me that a detective had questioned her, and she'd given him my name. She was pretty sure I'd get a similar visit and wanted to apologize for dragging me into it."

Thanks Mom, I thought. *Warning the suspect in advance is always helpful.*

I was sure Karen had the same reaction, but she kept her demeanor steady. "I see. Well then, what can you tell us about Connie's relationships with them?"

Leslie fidgeted impatiently. "You already know all this. Salton harassed her and drove her to suicide. Lowell prepped her for it by seducing her when she was still an undergraduate. I hated both of them for what they did to her."

That certainly fit what we expected, but if she really was the killer, I couldn't believe she'd have spoken so readily. Unless it was a bluff, and she wanted us to conclude she was innocent precisely *because* she was making herself look guilty.

Karen still maintained a noncommittal expression. "They were both murdered recently. What can you tell us about that?"

Leslie actually grinned. "The bastards deserved it. But I didn't kill them, if that's what you're asking."

"Why would you think that?" Karen asked.

"Why else would you be here? How dumb do you think I am?"

I was tempted to tell her that she must be pretty dumb to display such blatant hostility, but Karen spoke first. "Okay then, where were you on the evening of April twenty-seventh?"

"The night Salton was killed? I was at the cancer meeting in Boston, right where he was. I even heard his damn award lecture. But I still didn't kill him."

"Why were you at the cancer meeting?" I asked. "You work on the molecular biology of aging, right?"

She looked down her nose at me. "Cancer *is* a disease of aging. I thought even you cops knew that much."

I stifled a laugh and thought about telling her who I was. And that, while what she said was true, scientists working on aging didn't generally attend cancer meetings.

But Karen went on to her next question. "And how about the late afternoon of May twenty-sixth, when Steve Lowell was killed?"

"At home. I wasn't feeling well and went home around noon that day. And before you ask, I live alone."

So she hated both Salton and Lowell and had no alibi for either murder. Pretty strong suspect, except for the way she seemed so eager to admit everything up front.

Karen's frown told me that she agreed. "Would you be willing to let me swab your cheek for DNA? I'm sure you realize that you don't have verifiable alibis, and given the way you feel about the victims, we have to consider you a suspect. We recovered DNA from the crime scene, so DNA analysis would be the easiest way to establish your innocence."

Leslie snorted contemptuously. "More like establish my guilt, is what you're hoping! But sure, go ahead. Connie's mom told me that's probably what you'd do, so let's get it over with."

Karen went ahead and swabbed her cheek. After telling her that we'd brought a portable analyzer and would get the results in about an hour, we waited in the hall outside the microscope room.

Neither of us was surprised when Leslie's DNA didn't match the killer's.

———

"That was disappointing," I said, when we were back in the car. "She seemed like the perfect suspect at first."

Karen rolled her eyes. "Little bitch was just playing with us. She knew she wouldn't match the crime scene DNA, and that would clear her in the end. In the meantime, she was having some fun at our expense."

I groaned. "Well, so much for our latest lead. Any idea where we go from here?"

"I guess we're back to looking for someone else Connie was close to. Zelen may have gotten some names from her mother, and we'll be able to find more by going through Connie's social media accounts, texts, phone records, photos . . . all the stuff she had online."

"And what if that doesn't pan out any better than Leslie did?"

She threw up her hands. "Damned if I know. Connie's the only connection we have between Salton and Lowell. Do you have some other thought? You've got that look you get when you're playing with something in your head."

"I'm not sure. But you and Zelen are basing everything on the assumption that the killings were motivated by Salton's being a sexual predator, which was somehow connected to Lowell."

"And you don't think that's correct?" There was a hint of impatience in her voice. "We only know two things for sure in this damn case. That Salton was a predator with multiple victims, and that he and Lowell were killed by the same person. What else do you think could be going on?"

"The fact that there's just one killer is indisputable, and that clearly implies a link between Salton and Lowell. But it's a separate assumption that the underlying motive was Salton's sexual misconduct."

"True. But sexual harassment and intimidation are damn good motives for a revenge killing. What are you thinking? Come on, spit it out already."

"Just that we don't seem to be getting anywhere. So maybe it's time to check our premises."

"Didn't 'check your premises' come from Ayn Rand's *Atlas Shrugged*?" Karen asked.

"It did. And Einstein said something similar. As did Robert Parker's Jesse Stone. I believe his line was, 'If you don't like the answers you're getting, check your premises.'"

Karen managed a half smile. "That's an interesting assortment of sources. And Jesse Stone is my favorite fictional detective, so I guess I have to follow his advice. You're suggesting that the killings are based on something other than sexual misconduct? How else are Salton and Lowell connected?"

"Professionally. They're both cancer docs."

"True. But how does that translate into a motive for murder?"

"It could still come down to revenge. No matter how good a physician is, advanced cancers are usually not curable. The best we can do is hold them in check, and many patients ultimately die from their disease."

I could almost see the lightbulb go off in Karen's head. "Got it! And the relatives or friends of those patients might blame the physician for not having saved their loved ones. Meaning we should look for *patients*, not students, that Salton and Lowell had in common. And whose relatives or friends might be out for revenge."

I shrugged. "Seems like it might be worth a try."

"You're right, it sounds plausible. Do you think Lowell and Salton might have worked together and treated the same patient?"

"No, Lowell told me that he and Salton never collaborated. But both Lowell and Salton were lead investigators on multiple clinical trials, so it's certainly possible that a patient treated by one of them subsequently volunteered for a trial run by the other."

"And if that patient wound up dying, someone out for revenge might decide to go after both docs." Karen finished my thought. "It works for me. I'll ask Zelen to get a list of Salton's patients and have my guys pull Lowell's. Then we can look for matches. Not bad thinking for an amateur detective, Professor!"

I gave her a wink. "Thanks, Lieutenant."

I decided it was better not to mention another possibility that had occurred to me. If it were true, it wouldn't help Karen track down the killer, so there wasn't any point.

CHAPTER 24

When nothing useful emerged from further investigations of Connie Hillyard's friends and relatives, Karen and Zelen shifted their efforts to focus on patients Salton and Lowell had had in common. Teams of detectives from both Maine and Massachusetts spent the last week compiling lists of patients that both docs had treated. The detectives still weren't quite finished, but so far they'd identified three patients of Salton's who'd participated in clinical trials run by Lowell and five patients of Lowell's who'd been in trials directed by Salton. Six of those eight were deceased, and interviews of their families and friends were getting started.

In the meantime, I had actual science to keep me busy. An email from the editor of *Natural Science and Medicine* brought good news.

Dear Dr. Parker:

We have completed the full review of your paper, Increased Efficacy of Double-Antibody ADCs for Lung Cancer Treatment, *and I have attached the comments of three expert referees. I am pleased to note that all three recognize the importance of your results and consider your paper, in principle, to be suitable for publication in* Natural Science and Medicine.

I would be happy to consider a revised version of your manuscript that responds to the reviewers' criticisms. Most importantly, two of the three referees indicate that your experiments need to be extended to tumor explants from additional patients. While recognizing the importance of these results, indeed because *of their importance, they argue that the sample size for these studies should be at least twice the number you've used. Compliance with this recommendation would be necessary for the manuscript's eventual acceptance and publication.*

Thank you again for the opportunity to consider your work.

Jerome Blackwell, Editor

When I looked over the reviewers' comments, I was delighted to see that, except for increasing the number of patient explants, they were all straightforward and easily dealt with by some minor rewriting. We'd realized that the reviewers might ask us to extend our studies to a larger sample of explants, so Ginger had begun working on that right after we submitted the manuscript. By the time we heard from the editor, she'd completed experiments with eight additional explants, and studies of six more were ongoing.

Earlier this morning, she'd shown me the results for the full set of fourteen. They were fully consistent with the first ten in the original manuscript, with a response rate of nearly 80 percent to the double-antibody ADC. So we now had results with explants from twenty-four patients in total—four more than the reviewers had requested. Ginger had already updated the manuscript, and I was just finishing my cover letter to the editor when there was a knock at the door, and Carolyn Gelman came in.

"Hi, Brad. You're looking happy this morning."

"I am happy," I acknowledged. "I'm just about to send Ginger's revised paper back to *Natural Science and Medicine*. Where I'm sure this version won't have any problem being accepted."

She extended her arm for a congratulatory handshake. "That's great! You got the experiments with more explants done?"

"Yep. And the results look terrific. The double-antibody ADC is twice as effective as either of the single-antibody ones."

"Fabulous! Well, I won't keep you long. You should send back the paper and take Ginger out to lunch to celebrate. But I wanted to let you know that we're ready to begin enrolling patients in the trials, and I think we should notify oncologists around the state so we can start getting referrals."

"Good idea. Do you want to send out an email?"

"No, I think it should come from you. It can just be a brief cover letter, and we can attach the protocols." She handed me a sheet of paper. "I drafted something, if you want to use it."

Dear colleagues,

I'm writing to let you know that we are beginning phase I/II trials of two promising new drugs. The first is a double-antibody ADC developed in my lab, and the second is a selective inhibitor of oncogenic RAS mutants developed by Carolyn Gelman's group.

Both trials will enroll patients with advanced lung cancer. All such patients are eligible for the double-antibody ADC trial, and patient biopsies will be tested for the appropriate RAS mutation to determine eligibility for the selective inhibitor trial.

Protocols for both trials are attached, and we would be happy to share preclinical data or answer additional questions about either treatment.

Please contact Carolyn Gelman (cgelman@mtri.edu), medical director for both trials, with regards to patient referrals.

Brad Parker, Director, Maine Translational Research Institute

"Looks fine to me," I said. "Is it okay with you if I just use it as is?"

She pulled out her phone. "Sure. I'll send it to you so you won't have to retype it. Just copy and paste it into your email and hit send."

"Consider it done. Think I should send it to the MTRI distribution lists as well? Just to let everyone know what's going on."

"Why not? People like to know what's happening at the institute."

"Okay, will do. While you're here, can I ask you about something else?"

"Of course, what's up? I thought you were in a hurry to get your paper back to *Natural Science and Medicine*."

"I am, but I've had to learn multitasking in this job. I've been thinking about Penny and why she gets so upset at the idea of controls in clinical trials. Did you have a chance to talk to her after our last meeting?"

Carolyn nodded. "I did. She was very apologetic, said she just lost control. But I think I understand it a bit better now. She had a twin brother who died of leukemia two years ago. He was treated at a community hospital in rural Alabama, and she doesn't think he got very good care. So the idea of control patients who don't get the best possible treatment brings it all back and really bothers her."

I sighed. "Poor Penny. I can see why this is so hard for her. Does she understand at all why the controls are necessary?"

Carolyn shrugged her shoulders. "Sort of. But she argues if we already know that the new drug is significantly better, a control group shouldn't be needed. It just amounts to forcing half the patients to get an inferior treatment. She used your double-antibody ADC as her example this time, and it's hard to argue with Ginger's data on patient explants. If it works that well in phase two, she maintains there's no need for a control group in phase three."

"I can see her argument, although I'm sure the trial would be stopped early if the results go in the right direction. And now that you've told me about her brother, I understand why her response is so emotional. Do you think she should get help dealing with it?"

"I suggested that," Carolyn said. "Not that she's wrong to feel the way she does, but that it would be better for her if she were able to control it. She said she's been in counseling since her brother died, and she'll raise the issue at her next session. Who knows, maybe it'll help."

CHAPTER 25

SHIRLEY

The rage hit as soon as she saw the subject line: "New MTRI Clinical Trials." She forced herself to stay calm as she quickly read the email, just carefully enough to verify that her suspicions were correct. Then she moved it out of her inbox to the "personal" folder so she wouldn't have to look at it again until the end of the day when she was in the privacy of her own home. But its significance was clear. Gelman was now the official replacement for Lowell.

The first thing she did when she got home was to get the knife out of its hiding place in her closet. Her old friend, always faithful and ready to go to work. Running her thumb over its serrated edge made her feel in control as she sat down and read the email again.

There was really no question about what she had to do. She needed more victims to fulfill her duty. Salton had to have been first, of course. And then Lowell became second when he showed up as a substitute for Salton. And now Gelman was going to replace Lowell. She fondled her knife. *Then so be it.*

Killing Gelman here, so close to home, would make this riskier than her previous missions. But, at this point, she was confident the cops had no idea what she was doing. The newspapers had reported that Salton was killed by a woman who'd picked him up in the lobby of his hotel. And Lowell was said to have been the unfortunate victim of a random mugging. There was nothing to cast suspicion on her, and she'd just have to keep it that way by coming up with a different scenario for Gelman.

Killing her at work was out. Too many people around. And catching her going to her car, like she'd done with Lowell, wouldn't work either. Parking at MTRI was in an open lot that was visible from nearly half the windows in the institute. There was no place to hide, nothing like the dark corner she'd been able to find in Portland.

That left killing her at home. So why not a home invasion gone bad? She'd just have to do some background legwork to figure out Gelman's living situation and plan everything out.

She started by checking social media and was pleasantly surprised to find that Gelman was at least moderately active on Facebook. She lived in Kennebunkport, just north of Wells. There were lots of pictures of two kids, a boy and a girl, who looked to be somewhere in their late tweens or early teens. Her relationship status was blank, and there was no mention of a husband, so she was probably divorced. Nor were there any pictures of other men, suggesting that she most likely lived alone with the kids. And an enormous black dog.

Could be worse, Shirley decided. But the kids were a problem. She couldn't very well fake a break-in and kill Gelman with the kids there. And killing innocent children was definitely not part of her playbook.

She mentally shrugged. She'd just have to watch Gelman for a while and establish her routine. There had to be times when she was home without the kids.

An internet search yielded Gelman's address on Ocean Avenue, about twenty minutes away. Shirley went there early the next morning and was surprised to find that Gelman lived in a luxurious-looking contemporary perched on a rocky cliff above the ocean. She didn't know what the price tag for a house like that would be, but it had to be worth a small fortune. Not something Gelman could afford on a professor's salary, so she figured it was probably part of a divorce settlement.

She parked down the street and watched until Gelman left with her kids a little after seven. She took them to the middle school in Kennebunk, dropped them off, and proceeded to MTRI. *Too bad,* Shirley thought. She'd hoped that the kids took the bus and Gelman would be home alone after they left. But if this morning was typical, that wasn't going to work.

Evenings didn't seem promising either. Shirley spotted her leaving the institute a few minutes before four. Leaving a safe distance between them, she followed Gelman back to the school. The kids were waiting for her, probably having been engaged in after-school sports or other activities, and home they all went. She waited another four hours outside the house, but that was it for the night.

The next three days were the same boring routine, with the only variation being the time she picked the kids up, presumably because there were different after-school activities on different days. *Whatever.* The only thing that mattered was that it seemed that whenever Gelman was home, so were the kids. Even though that couldn't be completely true, there didn't appear to be any regular time during the school week when she could count on catching Gelman home alone.

That left weekends, so she kept watch both Saturday and Sunday. Saturday morning started with Gelman and both kids getting into her car around ten. They drove to a house about a mile away, dropped the boy off, and then Gelman and the girl went to a nearby Hannaford to shop for groceries. Half an hour after they returned home, a car pulled up in front of the house, honked, and the girl came running out and hopped in the back where another girl, about the same age, was waiting.

Shirley perked up. Maybe this was a regular weekend routine. The kids off somewhere with their friends, leaving Gelman at home by herself. But no. Minutes after her daughter left, Gelman came out, got in her car, and drove into town. Shirley watched as she went to a CVS, followed by a stop at a liquor store, and finally a pet store. Maybe now she was going back home? But again no. She drove to the house where she'd left her son earlier, picked him up, and they went home together. A couple of hours later, Gelman went to pick up her daughter at another house in the neighborhood, and that was it until a little before six when a pizza delivery guy showed up with dinner. At that point, Shirley gave up in disgust and went to get something to eat herself.

She was back at her post on Sunday, but it turned out to be equally useless. This time, a friend of Gelman's son came to their house and stayed for a couple of hours. Then Gelman and both kids went out for lunch and an afternoon movie. And that was it. All three were home together afterward, and Shirley gave up around dinner time.

The only thing that looked like it might be a Gelman family routine was Sunday lunch and a movie, but that sure as hell wasn't going to do her any good. It would take planning and organization to pull off a fake home invasion. If she was going to do it, she needed a time she could count on, and she didn't see that happening.

Shirley was almost ready to alter her plan. But then she started to wonder whether Gelman's ex still had a place in the kids' lives. Judging from the house, she imagined him to be a successful professional. A divorced dad who'd have visitation rights and want to maintain contact with his kids. Maybe even take them on occasional weekends, leaving Gelman home by herself.

Of course, that might be imaginary nonsense. Maybe Gelman's

husband had died, and life insurance had paid for the house. Or maybe she was independently wealthy and had her kids by in vitro fertilization as a single mom. Or maybe the ex-husband lived in Japan. There were lots of maybes. But if she was right and there was an ex who visited his kids, one of those visits might be her chance.

CHAPTER 26

She figured the best way to find out if an ex was in the picture would be to get access to Gelman's email. If Gelman was divorced—and if her former husband was still part of the kids' lives—he and Gelman would need to schedule his visits. That would most likely be done, at least in part, by email. So if her assumptions held water, Gelman's email should contain exchanges with the information Shirley needed to schedule a visit of her own.

She didn't know how to get into someone else's email, but she found plenty of information online describing how hackers got email passwords. One approach was simply guessing. Some people used easy-to-remember generic things like "password" or "1234," while others used personal details, like the names of their kids or pets. It seemed unlikely that Gelman was that naïve, but since she had that kind of information from her Facebook page, she quickly tried a bunch of things. But no luck.

A more general approach, which most hackers used, was to infect the target's computer with malware, like a keylogger, that would record passwords and transmit them to the hacker. That sounded good, so Shirley delved deeper. Usually, keyloggers were included in attachments sent in phishing emails. If the attachment was opened, the keylogger would be installed. The problem was that everybody knew about phishing emails, and people were careful not to open attachments that came from unknown senders. She figured she could get around this by composing an email to Gelman that looked like it was from a physician referring a patient for one of the clinical trials. But there was still the risk that Gelman might try to follow up with the referring physician and realize it was a fake.

In her situation, she decided, a hardware keylogger was a better way to go. It wasn't an option for most hackers because it required physical access to the target computer. But that wouldn't be a problem for her. She'd just need to get into Gelman's office and install a small thumb drive-like device in Gelman's computer. Once installed, it could be accessed remotely, so she'd be able to retrieve the password and get into Gelman's email at her leisure.

Keyloggers were available on the internet at a price even she could easily afford, so she placed her order and would be ready to go in a few days. All she'd have to do was find a time when Gelman would be out of the office to install it.

The first opportunity conveniently came the day after her new keylogger arrived. There was an institute-wide seminar at noon that she was sure almost all faculty and students would attend. Most people didn't bother locking their offices or labs when they were just going to be out briefly during the middle of the day for something like a seminar. If that applied to Gelman, which Shirley thought it would, this would work.

A few minutes before noon, she positioned herself off to the side where she could keep watch on Gelman's office. Shortly before the seminar was scheduled to begin, Gelman went out and joined the flow of people headed toward the auditorium.

Shirley waited until the hall was empty. Then she left her post and went to Gelman's office. Just as she'd hoped, the door was unlocked. The computer was on, so she took a moment to see if Gelman's email was just sitting there open. Maybe she wouldn't even need the keylogger. But no, Gelman must have logged out when she left, so Shirley quickly installed the keylogger, left the office, and went to the auditorium, where the speaker was just getting started.

She managed to sit and appear to be listening attentively through the entire seminar, even though her mind was focused on what she'd find in Gelman's emails. When it was finally over, she hurried back to her desk and connected to the keylogger. Nothing, meaning Gelman hadn't logged on yet. Unless the keylogger wasn't working.

She spent several nervous minutes waiting, but then the keylogger came to life. Moments later it recorded what looked like an email password, and when Shirley tried it, she was in.

Gelman's email was organized into a dozen or so folders, with labels identifying most of them as containing professional correspondence like grants, manuscripts, reviews, institute memos, and so forth. But there were two that looked promising. One was labeled "Kids," and the other "Personal."

She started with "Personal." But it was just bills, paperwork about the house, orders from online vendors, and such. Nothing interesting.

She tried "Kids" next. That looked better. There were messages about school and all sorts of after-school activities, including dates and times. As well as emails between Gelman and her kids with arrangements for their visits to friends, movie dates, and so forth. It seemed like plans for visits with their father belonged here too, but there was nothing.

Perhaps there was no father, and hacking into Gelman's email had been a waste of time. Or maybe there was a folder with the father's name where she'd find what she was after. She scanned through the folders again, hoping to find one labeled with a man's name or maybe "Divorce" or "ex." But they all bore names with scientific connotations. Except for one labeled "Dumbass," which she assumed were stupid emails that for some reason Gelman hadn't simply deleted.

Or could Gelman have a caustic sense of humor?

She opened "Dumbass" and was immediately rewarded. It was filled with exchanges between Gelman and someone named Pete. The most recent, from two days ago, was just what Shirley needed.

This is my weekend with the kids. I'll pick them up Saturday morning at ten and return them Sunday afternoon around four or five.

To which Gelman had responded.

Okay, that'll work.

Shirley sat back with a satisfied smile. Killing time was almost here.

CHAPTER 27

She was prepared for action when she positioned herself to watch Gelman's house at nine forty-five Saturday morning. Her knife was ready and waiting in the tote bag, along with her laptop, a sandwich, some waters, and dog deterrent spray. She'd gotten a new disguise for the occasion and was convinced she'd be unrecognizable if she somehow got spotted or caught on a surveillance camera. She'd checked, and Gelman didn't have one, but you could never tell about a neighbor. She'd even rented a car and put on New Hampshire license plates she'd stolen from a grocery store parking lot in Portsmouth.

A black Mercedes SUV pulled up in front of the house at ten fifteen, and the kids came out carrying backpacks. Their father got out of the car and exchanged hugs with the kids. Gelman didn't come out of the house, and there was nothing said between her and her ex. He just got back in the car with the kids and drove away. Shirley figured it hadn't been a happy divorce, but then, not many were.

Finally, Gelman was alone. The question was, would she stay home or go somewhere? Shirley had plans for either contingency, but it would be easiest if Gelman went out, and she could get into the house while it was empty. So she watched and waited a bit longer.

Fifteen minutes later, Gelman backed her car out of the garage. Her dog was with her—Shirley could see its head in the back—which would make her job easier. She didn't relish the idea of breaking into a house with a dog standing guard. Especially not one the size of a small horse. If the dog was a problem when Gelman came home, she'd be able to control it with the deterrent spray.

She needed to know whether she had minutes or hours before Gelman returned, so she followed the car when it pulled away. When Gelman turned toward Wells, Shirley guessed she was going to work. Still, she followed her to MTRI in order to be sure. When she saw Gelman pull into the institute parking lot, Shirley turned around and headed back to Kennebunkport, confident that she'd have at least an hour or two before Gelman returned home.

This time, she parked in a public lot that was a mile or so away from Gelman's house and walked. When she reached the house, she snuck around to the back. As she'd suspected, there was a sliding glass door. Which turned out to be remarkably easy to open with the burglar tools she'd brought.

Once inside, she was impressed. Gelman's home looked like it had been professionally decorated in a coastal style, with luxurious and obviously expensive furniture and wall hangings. The ex must have money, as his Mercedes also vouched for.

She figured that a burglar looking for money or valuable jewelry would start with Gelman's bedroom, so she went upstairs. The master bedroom was obvious, and she started going through the dresser drawers, haphazardly scattering their contents around the room. She found some money under a pile of underwear, so she pocketed the cash and threw the assorted bras and panties on the floor. Another drawer contained a jewelry box, which she emptied onto the bed. She took a few expensive-looking pieces, including a diamond necklace that had to be worth a mint, and tossed the rest around the room. Then she surveyed her handiwork, knocked over a bedside table to add to the show, and went back down to the living room.

An armchair in the corner had a good view of the front door but was out of the line of sight of someone coming in, so she chose that for her perch and settled in to wait. She wasn't sure how long it would be before Gelman returned. Maybe an hour, maybe all day. But it didn't matter. She had plenty of food and water, as well as lots of reading material on her laptop.

And her knife was all ready to greet Gelman when she got home.

CHAPTER 28

BRAD

I was surprised to find Karen on the deck, drinking coffee and looking out over the ocean, when I woke up Saturday morning. We both typically went to work for at least part of the day on Saturday, but usually after a late start. I filled a mug with coffee for myself and went out to join her.

"You're up early this morning. In a hurry to get to work?"

She turned to look at me with a halfhearted smile. "I don't know if I should be, but yes. The last reports on interviews with relatives and friends of patients who were treated by both Salton and Lowell made it to my desk last night. We've got nothing so far, so I'm anxious to go over these. There's got to be something there. If not, I don't know where we go next. Other than the damn cold case file."

"I'll keep my fingers crossed for you. I've had one other idea, but I haven't said anything because it won't take you anywhere."

"May as well let me in on it. At least it'll give me something to think about if the new reports are just more duds."

I took a sip of coffee and decided it wouldn't hurt to plunge ahead. "All right here goes. What I'm thinking is that maybe the killer is neither a former patient nor a former student of Salton and Lowell."

Karen knit her brow. "I don't get it. You're considering some motive other than revenge?"

"No, I still think revenge is key. And that the connection between Salton and Lowell is their prominence as clinical cancer investigators. But what if they weren't targeted as specific individuals? Maybe the killer is out for revenge against cancer docs as a group."

She frowned and shook her head. "That doesn't make sense. Cancer docs help people. Even if they don't always succeed, at least most of them do the best they can for their patients. Or don't you agree?"

"No, I'm sure you're right. Although there are undoubtedly some incompetent physicians around. But Salton and Lowell didn't just treat patients, they ran clinical trials. And before a new drug can be approved, it has to be shown to be more effective than the current best treatment. In order to do that definitively, one group of patients in the trial gets the new drug, while a second gets the drug that's currently used. Sometimes the new drug works better, but sometimes not."

Karen nodded slowly. "I think I get it. However the trial turns out, one group of patients didn't get the best treatment. And those patients got sicker or maybe died when perhaps they could have been helped."

"Exactly. And patients don't get to choose which treatment they receive. Assignment to the test group or the control group is made randomly," I added.

"So it'd be easy for a survivor to blame the physician running the trial if their loved one didn't get whichever treatment turned out to be the best. Even though the doc didn't know in advance. But to go from that to killing *anyone* who runs clinical trials?" She shook her head. "That's hard to buy."

"It's certainly far beyond reason," I agreed. "But impossible?

I'm not so sure. Remember Carolyn's student, Penny? The one I told you got all upset when Lowell talked to us about the design of clinical trials."

"I do. And I see where you're going. Her reaction was pretty off the wall."

"She did the same sort of thing when Carolyn and I met with our students to discuss running the trials ourselves after Lowell was killed. Carolyn talked to her afterward and came away with some understanding of what was going on. Penny had a twin brother who died of leukemia after receiving lousy care, and the idea of patients not receiving the best treatment seems to be all it takes to elicit an irrational response."

Karen nodded but didn't say anything further. Which I knew meant she was thinking things through.

After a few minutes, she spoke again. "I get what you're saying, but I think there's a variant that I like better. Rather than being totally random, what if the first killing—Salton—was specifically targeted."

"Meaning the killer was avenging a loved one who was in one of Salton's trials?" I asked.

"Mm-hmm. But killing Salton felt good, and she decided not to stop with him. There were other docs who ran trials and deserved the same fate."

"And she chose Lowell next because of his prominence," I finished her thought. "If that's right, it suggests that our killer has ties to someone who died after being in a trial Salton ran. You've looked at relatives and friends of patients who were treated by both Salton and Lowell. Can you go back and just consider Salton's patients?"

She laughed mirthlessly. "How many patients do you think that would be?"

It only took me a minute to realize how stupid my suggestion was. Phase III trials consisted of hundreds of patients, and Salton had run at least a dozen.

"Sorry, that was really dumb," I admitted. "It has to be well over a thousand."

"Far too many for us to deal with. Which means that if this line of thinking is right, we're left with no place to go. And with one chilling expectation."

I knew what she was thinking. And it made my spine tingle.

"That our killer's not finished," I said.

CHAPTER 29

I was surprised to see Carolyn's car in the MTRI parking lot when I got to work. She reserved weekends for her kids rather than coming to the institute, although she always took things home to work on. I hoped that this break in her routine wasn't due to adding the new clinical trials to her responsibilities. If it was, I'd have to figure out how to shoulder more of the work.

I stopped by my lab and briefly chatted with the two students who were there. Then I went down the hall to Carolyn's office, where I found her at her desk and Molly lying in her bed on the floor. After greeting Molly, I sat down across from Carolyn.

"Seeing your car in the lot took me by surprise. What are you doing here on a weekend? I thought this was kid time."

She grinned. "Aren't I allowed to deviate from routine?"

"Only with the director's prior approval," I replied with a straight face. "But seriously, I hope you're not so overburdened with the clinical trials that you had to come in on a Saturday morning."

"No, they haven't posed a problem. But thanks for asking. The kids are in Portland with their father this weekend, so I figured I may as well use the time to catch up on some things here that I usually just ignore."

"All right, in that case, you have my permission," I teased. Then I noticed a big card on her desk. "What's this? Looks like a birthday card."

"It is. The kids made it for me and stuck it in my bag, so it came in with me this morning. Cute, huh?"

"Very. Gail seems to be quite the budding artist. But is this your birthday? And you're all alone for it?"

She shrugged. "Yep, another year under the old belt. Pete scheduled this weekend with the kids months ago, and I didn't even think about it. Bobby asked him to change it when he realized it was my birthday, but Pete, of course, refused. Too busy and all that crap. And before you ask, Martin's stuck at a department retreat, so he couldn't come up either."

Carolyn and my old friend Martin, whom I'd known since graduate school, had become an item over the last year. They'd met when Martin, who was then a dean at Yale, had offered her a job that an alternative candidate wanted badly enough to kill for. Literally. In the end, he'd kidnapped Carolyn's children to force her to turn down the position, and the four of us—Martin, Karen, Carolyn, and I—wound up in a gun battle with his hired thugs. Martin's quick reflexes coupled with his experience as an Army Ranger in Iraq had saved Carolyn's life, and it didn't come as much of a surprise that they bonded after that.

"That's too bad. It would have been a nice chance for the two of you to spend a couple of days together without the kids," I remarked. "So you're all alone?"

"It's no big deal. Birthdays come and go. I'll fix myself a nice dinner and watch a movie tonight to celebrate."

———

I had a different thought walking back to my office. And it might cheer Karen up a bit too, assuming her last look through the reports on potential suspects turned out to be another disappointment.

I could tell from her tone of voice that she could use some cheering up as soon as she answered my call. Which she quickly confirmed when I asked how things were going.

"Shitty. There's nothing useful in these last interviews. Leaving us with your new idea, which amounts to looking for a microscopic needle in the world's biggest haystack."

"Well, maybe I can help take your mind off the case for a bit. Turns out that Carolyn's here at the institute because Pete has the kids this weekend. And today's her birthday."

"So is Martin coming up? A weekend alone would be nice for the two of them."

"Apparently not. He's at a department retreat and can't get away," I explained.

"You mean she's all alone for her birthday? That sucks."

"Yep. So I was thinking, why don't we surprise her and take her out for a nice dinner? Might make you feel better too."

"Good idea, Professor! Sometimes you display rare flashes of genius."

I chuckled. "Thanks, Lieutenant, glad you noticed. Let's plan on getting to her place around five. If she's there, we can have a drink before going out. If she's not home yet, we can let ourselves in and do a surprise happy birthday when she shows up."

CHAPTER 30

SHIRLEY

She'd been sitting and waiting for Gelman to come home for over six hours, and she was bored stiff. The reading material on her laptop had long since been exhausted, she'd eaten as much of her sandwich as she could get down, and all there was left for her to do was sit and stare at the door. At least running her finger over the blade of her knife helped her focus on the satisfaction to come.

But it wasn't even five o'clock. What if Gelman went out to dinner and didn't return for several more hours? Or even worse, what if she spent the night with a boyfriend and didn't come home until tomorrow when the kids were due to be dropped off? If she and the kids arrived at the same time, the whole plan would be blown.

But no, Shirley assured herself. Gelman would at least return early enough to settle in before the kids came home. And that would give her all the time she needed.

She just had to wait it out. But she could release some of her pent-up energy and have a little fun instead of just staring at the door. She'd messed up Gelman's bedroom and taken some valuables, but there was no reason to think that someone breaking in would leave the rest of the house in mint condition. A bit of random vandalism wouldn't hurt.

With a grim smile, she took her knife and attacked the cushions on the living room couch. Then she went after a couple of the pictures hanging on the walls and threw them to the floor. *This is much better than just sitting*, she thought, as she turned her attention to the dining room.

But just as she was about to tear into the upholstered dining room chairs, the doorbell rang.

She froze. If whoever it was saw her or noticed the damage she'd done, they'd call the cops. But maybe they wouldn't notice anything and just go away when there was no answer. She decided to wait and see, when the visitor knocked loudly and called out, "Carolyn, are you there?"

The voice sounded familiar, but before she had time to figure out who it belonged to, they yelled again, louder this time. "Carolyn, it's Brad and Karen. We're coming in."

She recoiled in shock. *Parker! Maybe with his girlfriend?* She'd heard the girlfriend was a cop, so she'd probably be carrying a gun. Which was more than her knife could handle.

She squeezed against the dining room wall, trying desperately not to be seen. And then she saw the doorknob start to turn. *They have a goddamned key!* And once they were inside, they couldn't help but notice the damage in the living room. She turned and hurried through the kitchen toward the back door, moving as quickly and quietly as she could.

But almost immediately, she heard the woman exclaim, "Brad, someone's been in here! Stay behind me in case they're still in the house."

Shirley turned for a quick look and was horrified to see them heading through the living room toward her, a gun in the woman's hands. She turned and ran for the door. But that gave her away.

"There they are!" the woman yelled. "Stop, police! Stop or I'll shoot!"

She couldn't let herself be taken. She raced through the door, shoved a barbecue grill in front of it to slow them down, and ran across the backyard as fast as she could. She heard a shot ring out behind her, but guessed it had to be a warning. She didn't think the woman would shoot her in the back, not if they thought she was just a vandal.

Luck was on her side. Before she'd gone too far, she heard a crash and a scream behind her. When she turned for a quick look, Parker was on the ground, apparently having fallen over the grill and hurt his leg. The woman was trying to help him, while he was pushing her away, yelling that he was fine and she should go after the intruder.

Shirley breathed a sigh of relief and continued racing to her car. This sucked, but tomorrow would be another day.

CHAPTER 31

BRAD

Karen helped me limp back into the living room. "I just twisted my ankle; it'll be fine," I kept saying. "I can walk on it already. You should've kept going, you could have caught whoever it was."

She shrugged. "No big deal, probably just a kid looking for pocket money. Why don't you sit down on the couch and rest your foot for a few minutes? I'll take a look around."

It was only when we got over to the couch that we realized how badly it was damaged.

"If it was a neighborhood kid, it was a damn destructive one," I remarked.

Karen bent over to examine the slashes more carefully. "And one who had a good size hunting knife. Put your foot up on the coffee table while I go see what it looks like upstairs."

She'd just gotten up the stairs when Carolyn and Molly came through the front door. When Carolyn saw someone sitting on the couch, she gasped and went rigid. Molly's reaction was simpler— she came running over, started licking me, and hopped up on the couch. When Carolyn realized who I was, she relaxed and started laughing at Molly's antics. "What are you doing here, Brad? You scared the crap out of me. Good thing Molly recognized you."

"Sorry, didn't mean to frighten you. Karen's here too, by the way. Upstairs."

I was about to tell her what was going on when she noticed the damage to her living room. "What the hell! What happened to the couch?! It looks like somebody shredded it."

"We came to surprise you and take you out for your birthday, but an intruder was in the house when we got here. We tried to grab them, but they made it out the back and got away."

"And that's who cut up the couch?" Carolyn asked. "And the artwork on the floor over there?"

I turned and noticed that for the first time. "Afraid so. I'm sorry about the damage."

Karen must have heard us and come back downstairs. "They also ransacked your bedroom. You better come up and take a look."

I followed Carolyn upstairs, ignoring the sharp pain in my ankle when I put weight on my left leg. It looked like her bedroom had been searched, with some of the contents of her dresser thrown around the room. But there was no wanton destruction like we'd found downstairs.

"Can you tell if anything's missing?" Karen asked. "I think they were looking for something in here. Especially in your dresser."

"I don't have much that would interest a burglar, but I do keep a couple hundred in cash hidden in my underwear drawer. And I have a few pieces of jewelry that are probably worth some money."

"It looks like your underwear is on the floor over there," Karen noted.

Carolyn grunted as she went over to the pile and looked through it quickly. "The cash is gone. But at least it was only a few hundred."

"How about the jewelry?" Karen pointed to the bed. "Is that your jewelry box?"

"Mm-hmm. And it looks like most of my jewelry is scattered around on the floor. Let me do a quick inventory."

Carolyn spent a few minutes going around the room and collecting the jewelry she found. "I can't be completely sure, but I think it's all here except for the couple of valuable pieces I had. A diamond necklace, an emerald ring, and a pair of diamond earrings are definitely missing."

"Ouch," Karen said. "Sounds like our thief knew what to take. Are those pieces insured?"

Carolyn shrugged. "I don't know. Doesn't matter. They were all gifts from that bastard Pete. I never wore them, and I never would have. How about my office and the kids' rooms? Were they ransacked too?"

"No. This is the only room up here that was touched," Karen replied. "They must have figured this is where they'd find any valuables."

I was bothered by how different this looked from the extensive damage that had been done in the living room. "The difference between this and downstairs seems odd, doesn't it? The intruder seems to have made an organized search up here, taken what they wanted, and left. No slashing or wholesale destruction like they did in the living room."

"It seems strange to me too," Karen agreed. "Almost as if a different person was responsible, except we only found one intruder when we got here."

She went over to where a small table was lying on the floor and picked up an alarm clock. "Carolyn, what time did you leave the house this morning?"

"It was around ten thirty. Why?"

Without answering, Karen held up the alarm clock. "Does this work?"

"Yeah. I keep it on my bedside table so I can look at the time if I wake up during the night. What's going on?"

"It's not working now," Karen observed. "I assume because it got unplugged when the table was knocked over. And it reads eleven twenty-two."

"So the intruder ransacked this room shortly after eleven," I remarked. "And they were still in the house when we got here a little after five. Why would they hang around for six hours like that? Or are you thinking it might have been someone different when we came in?"

"No. Two different people breaking in on the same day would be far too coincidental," Karen said. "And the only reason for someone to hang around—"

I saw where she was going and finished her sentence. "Would be to surprise Carolyn when she returned home. And maybe when they got tired of waiting, they took out their frustration on the living room."

Karen nodded. "That's what I'm thinking. Do you remember what I said about the slashes in the sofa?"

It took a moment for it to come back to me. When it did, I felt sick with fear.

But before I could speak, Carolyn interrupted. "Will one of you tell me what the hell you're talking about?"

"Let's go back downstairs first," Karen said. "I need to take another look at the damage to your couch."

CHAPTER 32

Karen knelt down by the couch and examined several of the slashes. Then she took out her gun and stuck the barrel into three places where the couch had been stabbed instead of slashed. It took me a moment to figure out that she was using her gun as a ruler to measure the depth of the holes.

She looked up with a sigh. "The knife that did this had a six-inch serrated blade."

"Like the knife that killed Salton and Lowell," I added, the knot of fear in my stomach tightening.

Carolyn looked at us open-mouthed. "What are you saying?! You don't think those killings have something to do with me, do you?"

Karen and I exchanged glances. When she nodded, I took Carolyn's hand and answered. "I'm afraid we do. It looks like the killer was here and planned to make you the next victim."

The color drained from her face. But then she rallied. "Wait a minute, that doesn't make any sense. You said the killer was somehow connected to both Salton and Lowell. Either a student

Salton harassed, or a relative of a patient they'd both treated. Why would they suddenly come after me?"

Karen shook her head. "That was our thinking, but it hasn't held up. We've looked at everyone who fit into those groups without identifying a single viable suspect. So now we're thinking that the killer might be targeting cancer docs more generally. Maybe she started with a specific target in Salton. Killing him felt good, and she expanded the field after that."

"That's crazy!" Carolyn protested. "It'd be totally insane for somebody to simply kill cancer docs."

"No argument that it's crazy," Karen replied. "But you were supposed to be number three, which would have made her a serial killer. And 'crazy' is a perfectly apt description for serial killers."

"We don't think it's cancer docs in general, though," I put in. "More likely, she's specifically targeting cancer docs involved in clinical trials. The idea is that the killer had a friend or relative who died after being in a trial, possibly in a control group. The killer blames the trial director for not giving her loved one the best possible treatment and is out for revenge. Maybe it was one of Salton's trials, and he was the killer's initial target. Lowell was next because of his prominence in the field."

Carolyn frowned. "I don't buy it. Okay, I'll grant you revenge as a motive for Salton. But it makes no sense to generalize that to a global campaign against all clinical trial directors. It's completely irrational."

"Again, no argument," I said. "But an irrational response to a loved one's death isn't out of the question. Look at how your student Penny goes bananas at the idea of control groups in clinical trials, simply as a reaction to her brother not having received the best care for his leukemia. And he wasn't even in a trial."

Carolyn was quiet for a long minute, and I could tell what I'd said about Penny was sinking in. Then she nodded slowly. "All right, I see where you're coming from. But if the killer's targeting clinical trial directors, why me? I don't have any reputation in that field."

"But you're stepping in to run the trials of your and Brad's new drugs," Karen pointed out. "That could have put a target on your back, especially since you're taking Lowell's place. And if that's it, the list of potential suspects becomes much smaller. Just the people at MTRI who know what you guys are planning, right? That can't be more than a dozen or so; we can just ask them to volunteer for DNA tests."

Karen's eyes were glowing with excitement at the prospect of finally identifying the killer. I hated to do it, but I had to bring her back to reality.

"I'm afraid it's not going to be that easy," I said. "We sent out an email announcing the trials to all of the hospitals and oncology groups in Maine, asking for patient referrals and identifying Carolyn as the clinical director. It was a long list of recipients, and we copied it to all MTRI faculty, staff, and students. Plus, who knows how many primary recipients forwarded it on to other colleagues."

"That seems to have happened pretty widely," Carolyn added. "I've received inquiries from physicians in several other states, including New Hampshire, Vermont, and Massachusetts."

The excitement left Karen's face as we were speaking. "There goes my hope of a quick and easy solution. But maybe there's another angle. Carolyn, how many people knew you were going to be alone, without the kids, today?"

"Just Pete. I didn't have any reason to tell anyone, so I didn't. Not even Martin, so that he wouldn't feel guilty about going to his department retreat. Why?"

"Because I think the killer knew," Karen said. "She ransacked your bedroom no more than an hour after you left, and then she was waiting for you to come home. Her choice of a day when the kids were away can't just be random. I think she planned it to get you alone because she didn't want to hurt them."

Carolyn took a deep breath. "I guess the silver lining is that she wasn't after the kids. But how would she have known they were out of the house?"

"How do you make visitation arrangements with Pete? Do you use phone or email?" Karen asked.

"Email. I try not to talk to the bastard if it can be avoided."

Karen nodded. "Doesn't surprise me. I'll bet the killer hacked your email."

Carolyn shook her head. "I don't think so. I'm paranoid about phishing emails."

"You never click on links or open attachments?"

"No. I always go to the website instead of following a link. And I don't open attachments unless it's something I'm expecting."

I wasn't surprised that Carolyn was cautious. But if I were trying to hack her email, I knew just how I'd go about it.

"How about responses to my email asking for referrals to our clinical trials?" I asked. "Did any of them come with patient records attached?"

Carolyn's eyes widened. "Shit! Of course, they did. And I opened them without a second thought. They all looked legit, but that's how I'd do it if I were a hacker."

"Me too. And if that's what happened, it had to be a recipient of my announcement email."

"Sounds right to me," Karen agreed. "Carolyn, is it okay if I send over one of our IT guys to see if they can find malware in your computer? Some kinds self-destruct without leaving evidence behind, but we might get lucky."

"Of course. If you did find something, would that lead us to the killer?"

"Probably not, but it would be useful to confirm Brad's suspicion," Karen replied.

"It won't really add anything, though," I commented. "Whether you find malware or not, the killer has to be one of the recipients of that email."

"True enough," Karen agreed. "Which still leaves us with a long list. There's something else we need to discuss, though. Carolyn, given what we know now, I think we have to seriously consider your student Penny as a possible suspect."

Carolyn's eyes flashed. "No way! She'd never do anything like this."

Karen held up a hand in a placating gesture. "Your students are like family, I get it. But you have to admit that the way she goes off at the idea of control groups in clinical trials is pretty irrational."

"Maybe, but she's not the only one who feels that way," Carolyn countered. "Just as an example, I ran into a group of people arguing about the issue while I was getting a glass of wine after Lowell's lecture. Two of them were vigorously asserting that it was unethical to withhold the best treatment from control patients."

"Do you know who they were?" Karen asked.

"One of them was Jackie Danielson. She works in Doug Samson's lab, just down the hall from mine. I don't know the other one."

"I'm sure they're just the tip of the iceberg, though," I said. "The ethics of controls in clinical trials is an issue that people debate, with reasonable arguments to be made on both sides. I suspect there are plenty of people at the institute who don't like the idea of using patients as controls. But the disturbing thing about Penny is how emotional she gets. She was obviously aware of Lowell's involvement in trials. Would she have known anything about Salton?"

"She probably knew who Salton was from having gone to the cancer meeting in Boston," Carolyn said. "But what triggers her is her brother's death from leukemia because he got lousy treatment in rural Alabama. He wasn't in a clinical trial, let alone one that Salton ran."

I understood Carolyn being protective of her student. It was a natural reaction, and I'd probably feel the same way if I were in her place. But I had to agree with Karen. Penny had become too strong a candidate to ignore.

"If Penny was at the meeting, she probably attended Salton's award lecture. It was a big event."

Carolyn glared at me. "Yeah, so what?"

"I was in the audience too. His talk was largely about his phase three trial of melistomab, and he emphasized how much better the experimental group fared than the controls. Don't you think that might have triggered Penny, just like we've seen happen in our own discussions?"

"I guess. But that doesn't make her a murderer!" Carolyn insisted, her face starting to flush.

"Of course not." Karen spoke calmly. "But I do want to talk to her and see if she has alibis for the times of the murders, as well as for today. And I want to get a DNA sample."

Carolyn shook her head firmly. "No, leave her alone. I'm sure she's not it, and she'll blame me if you approach her. It'll destroy our relationship, and she'll probably wind up quitting grad school. All because she trusted me enough to tell me about her brother."

Karen started to protest, but I held up a hand to stop her. "Hang on a minute. You wouldn't need to interview her if you had a DNA sample, would you? Maybe we could get that some other way." Then I turned to Carolyn. "Does Penny have a coffee cup in the lab? Or something else that would have her DNA on it?"

That broke the tension and Carolyn's expression relaxed. "She keeps a mug as well as dishes and a sweater in her desk. Would that work?"

Karen let out a deep breath. "That should be fine. We won't get enough DNA to do the rapid analysis I can do with a mouth swab, but I can get a sample from the cup and put it through the standard procedures at the crime lab. We'll have an answer in a couple of days. In the meantime, we'll follow up with Jackie Danielson."

"Good," I said. Then I turned to Carolyn again. "Now that that's settled, how about putting Karen and me up for the night?"

Karen immediately seconded the idea. "Absolutely, you shouldn't be alone until we figure this out. I'll get the unit to organize round-the-clock protective details for you starting tomorrow."

"You guys staying here tonight sounds great, thank you. But having protective details all the time will drive the kids nuts. Do you really think that's necessary once they're back home?"

I spoke up before Karen could answer. "Maybe there's a different solution, one that I'm sure the kids won't mind. Why don't we give Martin a call? I can guarantee he'll want to be here once he knows what's going on."

CHAPTER 33

Martin sounded breathless when he answered the phone. "Hey Brad, can't talk now. I'm running to the lecture hall before the session starts."

I laughed. Martin had been chronically late for as long as I'd known him. "Okay, call me back as soon as you can. We need your help with a situation Carolyn's in."

"Whoa, is there a problem? Speak. Won't be the end of the world if I'm a few minutes late."

"We think a killer came after her today. Karen and I chased them off before Carolyn came home. We're with her now, but—"

"Never mind, I got it. I'll be there ASAP."

"We'll stay with her tonight, Martin. Go to your session and come tomorrow."

"Screw that! See you soon. And ask Karen to have a gun for me."

———

The doorbell rang at twenty past eight. Carolyn ran to the door and fell into Martin's arms. When they finally paused for breath, she said, "You didn't have to come. I'm fine."

Martin snorted. "Oh, right. Brad tells me some sort of maniac is after you, and I'm going to stick around a stupid department retreat? Sure, what else would I do?"

Carolyn laughed and snuggled into his chest. "Well, when you put it that way."

Turning to me, he said, "Thank God you had the sense to clue me in. I'm not sure this one would have. Now, how about telling me what's going on."

We sat on the slashed-up couch, Carolyn poured drinks, and I took Martin through the whole story, starting with Salton's murder. He listened attentively, commenting only with headshakes and colorful expletives, until the end. Then he simply said, "You sure get yourself into some deep shit, old buddy. Damn good thing I'm here to help you out of it. Karen, you got that gun I asked for?"

She handed him a Glock that she'd retrieved from the box of supplies she kept in the back of her car. "Will this do?"

He took the weapon and smiled. "Nice. Same as the army issued to us Rangers in Iraq. Now, what's the plan? Do you think it's this gal Penny?"

Karen and Carolyn answered "Yes," and "No," simultaneously. Martin laughed. "Brad, looks like you have the deciding vote."

I shook my head. "I abstain. I agree with all of Karen's arguments, and Penny seems like the perfect suspect. But I also have to listen to Carolyn's take on her own student."

"Well, we'll know about Penny soon," Karen said. "Carolyn, can we go to your lab tomorrow morning and find her mug?" Carolyn nodded, and Karen continued. "Good. I'll swab it for DNA and take the sample straight to our lab. We should have the answer Monday or Tuesday."

"Martin or I should come too, so that Carolyn's not alone when you take the sample in for analysis," I added.

"Don't worry, she won't be alone until you get this sorted out," Martin asserted. "I'll take care of that."

Carolyn looked at him with a half smile. "Don't you have a job to get back to?"

"Nothing that I can't take some time off from. Remember, I'm not a dean anymore, thanks to our new president deciding to fire all the senior administrators appointed by his predecessor. I'm just a regular faculty member on sabbatical. And I'm staying right here until this maniac is dealt with."

I grinned and winked at him. "That's what I figured you'd want to do. Glad I called you."

Carolyn looked at me and then at Martin. Her eyes were bright. "Me too. And the kids will be thrilled to have you here. But it could be a long haul."

"I hope it won't be that long now," Karen ventured. "Even if it's not Penny, we can be sure it's someone who got Brad's email. We may know more Monday, when IT has a look at your computer. And we also have Jackie Danielson to check out. One way or another, we're getting closer."

"In the meantime, why don't the two of you get out of town?" I suggested. "Take the kids on a little vacation, without telling anyone where you're going. Carolyn, could they miss school for a bit?"

"They wouldn't have to. The school year ended last week. They're just going to be doing summer program stuff now."

"That sounds like a great idea then," Martin enthused. "Let's do it. I've heard that Bar Harbor's a fun place to visit."

"It is," I agreed. "Acadia National Park is gorgeous. Or you could go check out the mountains."

"Or how about Baxter State Park and the North Woods," Carolyn suggested. "The kids watched that TV show *North Woods Law* and loved it."

I laughed. "And we could go on. You've got plenty of choices; just don't tell anyone what you decide."

Martin smiled. "Glad you called me, old buddy. This is going to be more fun than I thought. Karen, don't feel like you have to be in a big hurry to solve the case."

Carolyn squeezed his hand. "Well, I don't know about that. Why don't you go ahead and nail your killer? We could continue our vacation anyway."

I got up and stretched. "Sounds good. I don't think you need Karen and me tonight, right?"

Martin winked and held up the Glock. "Nope, the three of us will be just fine alone."

CHAPTER 34

We got to MTRI at eight Sunday morning, figuring there wouldn't be many people around this early, and Karen would be able to swab Penny's coffee cup unnoticed. Carolyn's car was already in the parking lot, and we found her showing Martin her lab.

When he saw me, Martin grinned. "This isn't a bad-looking place. You seem to have done okay here."

I shrugged. "Not like your digs in New Haven, but we make do."

"Nice enough that you couldn't steal me away to Yale last year!" Carolyn teased him.

Karen turned the conversation to business. "C'mon, Carolyn, let's go find Penny's mug while nobody's around. I'm sure these two can entertain themselves for a few minutes."

"It's probably at her desk, right over here." Carolyn led the way to a desk on the side of the room, opened a drawer, and handed a mug to Karen.

Karen examined it and nodded in satisfaction. "Perfect. It obviously hasn't been cleaned since the last time she used it, so there should be plenty of DNA." She swabbed the mug and put the swab in a cardboard container. "Is that hairbrush hers too?" Carolyn nodded, and Karen swabbed the hairbrush as well.

"I'm going to run these up to the state crime lab in Augusta and push them to do the analysis ASAP. Brad, do you want to come for a ride? If not, I can either drop you at home first or pick you up here on the way back, probably eleven thirty or thereabouts."

I had work to do in my office but decided to go along for the ride anyway. It was nearly a three-hour round trip, so I thought Karen could use some company.

"And why don't the two of you come by my place when you get back?" Carolyn suggested. "The least I can do is take us all out for a nice lunch after everything you guys did yesterday."

"Good idea," Martin seconded. "You can help us plan our trip. I want to be sure we don't wander too far from the best restaurants."

I chuckled. Martin was perhaps the world's most ardent foodie. "Okay, I'll try to provide some guidance. You may have to duke it out with Carolyn and the kids, though—the North Maine Woods isn't known for gourmet dining."

———

Carolyn took us to a restaurant on Ocean Avenue, not far from her house. It was right on the Kennebunk River, and we got a table on the patio where we could sit and watch the boats go by. When Martin asked what was good, Carolyn unhesitantly recommended lobster, so we all followed her advice and ordered lobster rolls. Supplemented with Karen's suggestion of a plate of steamed soft-shell crabs to share on the side. And Martin's addition of Bloody Marys.

The drinks and food came quickly, and when Martin had tasted everything, he sat back with a satisfied smile. "Nice, I like it here," he proclaimed. "Brad, I trust you can produce a list of places this good for us to visit on our odyssey."

I winked at Karen. Martin's affinity for food was something she always got a kick out of.

"I'll give it my best shot," I promised. "Are there any other considerations that will go into planning your itinerary? You know, mundane things like places you want to see."

Martin kept a straight face as he replied. "Not really. Nothing as important as food, anyway."

Carolyn laughed and punched him in the shoulder. "You might have to check with the kids on that. But seriously, I don't want to stay home with the kids tonight, so we're going to leave after they get back this afternoon. That'll put us on the road around six, so we're not planning to go far before stopping for the night. I was thinking maybe somewhere around Portland."

"I know a nice resort on Cape Elizabeth," Karen suggested. "We went there for lunches a couple of times when I was in the Bureau's Portland office. It's right on the ocean and has a great beach. Called The Inn by the Sea, or something like that."

"Sounds interesting," Carolyn said. "The kids would probably love a day or two at a seaside resort. Do you think they take pets? I'd like to bring Molly."

"They do," Karen assured her. "I was surprised to see some really big dogs when we were there, so Molly'd fit right in."

Martin had finished his lobster roll and was about to spear the last crab, but he broke his rhythm for a moment. "And how about the important issue? How's the food?"

Karen rolled her eyes. "It's excellent. But I've always wondered, how do you ever get any work done when all you think about is food?"

Martin put down his fork and rubbed his chin. "Hmm, never thought about that. Do you think that's why they kicked me out as dean?"

I nodded gravely. "Yep, could have been a problem. But don't worry, Portland's famous as a foodie's city. You'll find some award-winning restaurants if you spend a couple of days there."

"Maybe that's what we should do," Carolyn remarked. "You'll know more tomorrow morning after IT checks out my computer. And still more when you get the DNA results back."

Karen nodded. "Which the lab promised they'd have by Tuesday. By then, we may also have talked to Jackie Danielson. So yes, a couple of days from now we may know quite a bit more."

Martin pushed back from the table with a satisfied look. "Sounds like staying around Portland and sampling a few of their eateries is a good idea. Then we can decide how long we want to be on the road and plan from there."

CHAPTER 35

K aren and I got to MTRI first thing Monday morning—
this time at seven—to meet her IT specialist. A few
people were already at work, but not Carolyn's students,
so nobody was curious about our visit to her office.

Carolyn had given me her password, and the IT guy spent over
an hour scanning her computer. Then he looked up with a shake of
his head. "No luck so far. I've looked in all the places malware
usually gets downloaded from phishing emails, and there's nothing. It could be hiding someplace else, but it'll take close to a day to
scan everything. Do you want me to take the computer back to the
office and run a full search?"

"Sure, do it," Karen said. "She's away on a trip, so taking the
computer's not a problem."

"Okay, I'll just disconnect it and get out of your hair." He went
around the desk to the back of the computer and started unplug-
ging the power cord and accessories. Suddenly he exclaimed,
"Holy shit!" and held up something that looked like a small flash
drive. "This little bastard's a hardware keylogger. Your hacker got

into the office and installed it in her computer. No phishing email needed. Should I take it?"

Karen shook her head. "No, leave it. I don't want the hacker to know it's been discovered."

———

When the IT guy left, Karen and I went back to my office. Anna had made coffee, so we filled a couple of mugs and sat at my conference table.

"That pretty much narrows the suspect list to someone who works here," Karen said. "I assume nobody from outside the institute could have gotten in and messed with Carolyn's computer?"

"No. The building's on a key card system after hours and monitored by video cameras to detect an unauthorized entrance. And Carolyn locks her door at night, so an intruder would have had to break into her office as well as getting into the institute."

"I'll have a crime scene unit check out the office, but I didn't see any signs of forced entry. How about when she leaves her office during the day? Does she lock it then?" Karen asked.

I shook my head. "We don't worry much about security during the day. I've gone back to her office with her after meetings or seminars lots of times, and the door's always unlocked."

"Then the most likely thing is that the keylogger was planted when Carolyn was out of her office during the day."

"Which points even more strongly to Penny," I noted. "Carolyn's office is right across the hall from her lab, so Penny was perfectly positioned to see when Carolyn left the office. Do you want to go ahead and question her? I'm sure Carolyn wouldn't object at this point."

"It's tempting, but there's no reason to do it just yet. And I don't want to risk tipping her off. Unless she were to suddenly confess, the bottom line would be getting a DNA sample, which we already have. If we're right, we'll be all set to arrest her tomorrow when we get the results. For today, I'm just going to have her watched to be sure that she doesn't panic for some reason and make a run for it. Do you think she's in the lab yet?"

I looked at my watch. Not quite nine. "Maybe, maybe not. I'll go see."

I found Penny at her desk and waved hello. When she asked if she could help me find something, I thanked her and said I was looking for Carolyn. A nice normal exchange with someone I was pretty sure was a murderer.

Karen looked relieved when I told her Penny was here. "Good. I was worried that she might have taken off after we almost caught her Saturday. I'll have someone posted outside the institute to keep watch. They can follow her when she leaves and stay on her to make sure she's still here for us tomorrow. Is there a picture of her on the MTRI website so they'll know what she looks like?"

"Sure, there are photos of all the students. Do you want to tell Carolyn about the keylogger or should I?"

"Let's hold off on that until tomorrow," Karen said. "There's no reason to tell her now, and it would just get her upset worrying about Penny. May as well wait until tomorrow when we know the answer."

CHAPTER 36

SHIRLEY

Her heart jumped when she saw Parker on Monday. Two days had passed since he and his cop girlfriend almost caught her at Gelman's house, and she was still a nervous wreck. She didn't think he'd seen her face on Saturday, and even if he had caught a glimpse, she'd been wearing a ton of camouflage makeup. Nonetheless, she spent Saturday night lying awake, expecting the police to come pounding at her door. By the time she woke up Sunday morning, she was ready to run but managed to hold it together long enough to think things through. And the more she thought about it, the more she convinced herself that neither Parker nor his girlfriend could identify her. Since she'd been careful not to leave fingerprints or DNA at the scene, there was also no way they'd be able to connect the break-in at Gelman's house to the Salton murder, where she knew she'd left plenty of DNA behind. They'd just conclude that she was a burglar who enjoyed a little malicious destruction on the side.

Repeating that litany got her through Sunday, but it didn't help when she first saw Parker this morning. She had to struggle to stay outwardly calm and not run for it. But he'd acted normally, without any sign that he recognized her from Saturday. So maybe, just maybe, she was safe.

Her confidence grew as the day went on and nothing happened. No odd visits from Parker, and no cops waltzing in to question her. It looked like she'd escaped repercussions from Saturday's debacle. Except that the mission had been a complete failure, and Gelman was still very much alive.

That had to be rectified. Whatever the danger to herself, the mission came first. But how to proceed after this abysmal failure?

The email Gelman had sent the lab on Sunday said that this week was the start of her kids' summer vacations, and she'd decided to take them on a family road trip. She thought they'd be gone for just a few days, but it might stretch to a week or more depending on how things went. In any case, she promised to keep in touch and asked everyone to email her with any exciting new results. Or, of course, if there were any questions or problems.

Nothing I can do while they're on a family road trip, Shirley decided. But the kids being on summer vacation should be helpful after they returned. It seemed reasonable to think that their father would take them for a week or two. Or maybe they'd go to an overnight camp for part of the summer. She hadn't found anything about those kinds of arrangements in Gelman's emails yet, but she'd continue monitoring them, as well as looking back over the last few months, in case plans had been made in advance.

She was sure there'd be some significant period of time when the kids would be away. What kids didn't spend a week or two visiting a divorced father during summer vacation? And if she had more advance warning and a longer period of time to work with, she'd be able to figure out a better plan than trying to stage a home invasion. Maybe doing it at the lab or when Gelman was leaving would work better. Or maybe Gelman would take advantage of the kids' absence and go on a trip herself.

Somehow, the right opportunity would come up. And this time she wouldn't blow it.

CHAPTER 37

BRAD

I was having a hard time concentrating on anything useful Tuesday morning. Karen fully expected to get the DNA results today and had promised to let me know right away. With that on my mind, I couldn't focus on normal business.

Was Penny really a double murderer, intent on making Carolyn her third victim if we hadn't interrupted her? She certainly hadn't acted like she had anything to hide when I went down to Carolyn's lab to check on her a couple of times yesterday and again first thing this morning. We'd just exchanged normal greetings. On the other hand, it was impossible to ignore her intense emotional reaction to discussions of clinical trials. Putting that together with the fact that Carolyn's computer had been hacked by someone with physical access made her a compelling suspect.

But if she really was the would-be killer Karen and I had interrupted, how could she be so cool with me now? I kept going over and over it in my head while I waited for the call from Karen that would provide the answer.

When I first arrived this morning, I noticed two black SUVs parked next to each other in the back of our lot. I didn't recognize them, so I assumed they were detectives waiting to arrest Penny as soon as Karen got the DNA results. I hoped they could carry out their task discreetly, but it probably didn't really matter. The news of Penny's arrest would race through the gossip mill and no doubt disrupt whatever else people were doing for days or weeks to come.

The cops hadn't moved when my phone rang with Karen's special ringtone. I was both surprised and pleased that she was calling me before ordering them into action. Grabbing the phone, I asked, "You got her?"

She answered in a dull voice. "No. It's not Penny."

"What?! Are you sure? Everything points to her."

"Of course, I'm sure. DNA doesn't lie."

I paused for a minute and watched the SUVs pull away. She must have told the detectives before calling me after all. But then I had another idea.

"DNA may not lie, but where it comes from might. What if somebody else used Penny's mug, and you have their DNA instead of hers?"

"Not a bad thought. But that's why I took a sample from Penny's hairbrush as well as from the mug. The two are identical."

"Shit! So we're back to square one?"

"I wouldn't go quite that far. Although I agree that we've suffered a setback. I was convinced it was Penny, too."

I took a deep breath and tried to mentally shift gears. "Yeah, I know. Okay, I'll text Martin the news, and he can tell Carolyn. That way, the killer won't see it."

"And tell Martin that Carolyn shouldn't change her password," Karen added. "I don't want to tip off the killer that we know what's going on. Carolyn should keep everything as is, just not send anything confidential over her email."

"Okay, got it. We can just communicate with her via Martin. But I don't know how long she's going to be able to stay in hiding. And

Martin won't be able to stay with her forever, as much as he might like to."

"I know. We'll just have to arrange protection for her and the kids when they come back."

"All right. Carolyn won't like it, but I guess that'll work. Meanwhile," I asked, "where do we go from here?"

"I'll start by having somebody talk to the woman Carolyn overheard arguing that control groups in clinical trials are unethical. Jackie Danielson. Maybe we'll get lucky. Why don't you wait until I get back to you on that before you text Martin?"

I tried to occupy myself shuffling routine paperwork while I waited to hear from Karen again. Which fortunately took less than an hour.

"Jackie Danielson's DNA is in the database," she began, "making it quick and easy to eliminate her."

"Because you already know nothing in your database matched the crime scene sample?" I asked.

"Right. But I had a detective talk to her anyway. And when he asked if she remembered the name of the other woman Carolyn overheard her talking to, he got an earful. That woman's name is Robin Holbrook, but Jackie also rattled off the names of another half dozen women who she knew were bothered by the way patients are used as controls. Like you said, it looks like the discussion Carolyn overheard wasn't unusual."

"I figured there'd be lots of people at MTRI with similar concerns about the ethics of control patients. Are you going to talk to the women Jackie identified?"

"May as well," Karen said. "But with the list growing this way, I don't think of them as strong suspects. So, I'm going to move ahead with a broader investigation at the same time."

"How are you thinking of proceeding? I sent the announcement email to all MTRI faculty, staff, and students. I don't have an exact count, but that has to be several hundred recipients."

Karen groaned. "I was hoping it wasn't that many. Well, we'll just have to try to work through them. I think our first approach is to compare your MTRI email lists with Zelen's list of patients who were in Salton's trials."

I was skeptical. "You'd have to be lucky for that to work. You'd only identify suspects who are relatives with the same surname as a patient."

"I know," Karen admitted. "We wouldn't pick up friends."

"And there are lots of relatives you'd miss too," I added. "For example, if the patient's a woman who changed her name when she got married, you wouldn't pick up her parents or siblings."

She sighed. "I hear you. And we could come up with lots more examples like that. But it's still worth doing because anyone who *did* show up would be a strong candidate."

"I guess there's no reason not to give it a try. But what if you come up empty after that? Do you think it'd be worth looking for people from the institute who attended the meeting in Boston where Salton was killed? We'd just have to go through the travel vouchers that were submitted for those dates."

"I thought about that, but it wouldn't really help," Karen said. "Our perp could have easily driven down to Boston for the evening to do the deed, so not going to the meeting wouldn't mean anything."

"Got it. So we have to hope that we get lucky, and the killer can be identified from the list of Salton's patients. I'm afraid that seems pretty chancy."

"I can't argue with that. But the only other thing I can think of doing is trying to get DNA samples from everyone at MTRI."

"From that many people!" I protested. "It'd be a long process, and once you start calling people in to collect samples, the killer'll figure out what's going on and run. The whole thing sounds like a logistic nightmare."

"You're right, it'd be a mess. But we've got to catch whoever's doing this, and I don't have any better ideas. Do you?"

I was starting to come up with one. But I wasn't about to share it with Karen. I could already hear her screaming objections at me.

CHAPTER 38

Martin answered the phone with a cheery, "Hey, Brad. This place is great. Dinner last night—"

I cut him off. "You can tell me about the food later. First let me fill you in on what's happened here."

I took him through finding the hardware keylogger in Carolyn's computer, the DNA evidence exonerating Penny, the outcome of interviewing Jackie, and Karen's plans for moving forward. When I finished, his response was straightforward and to the point.

"Shit. You'll have to be damn lucky for the killer to turn up as a patient's relative. And screening DNA from everyone in your institute? Karen's a smart lady, but that sounds sketchy as hell."

"I know. I'm afraid her chances are pretty slim, and I've started thinking of something different that I want to run by you. But first, what are you and Carolyn going to do now that we didn't get a quick answer? Have you talked about it?"

"Sure. Especially since Carolyn never thought Penny was the killer. I'd be happy hanging out with her and doing a tour of Maine, but she's anxious to get back to work. The kids love it here, so we can probably stay for a few more days, but then she'll want to head home. I'll stay at the house with her for protection, but I don't know how I'll be able to cover both her and the kids."

"I wish she'd go for your tour of Maine idea, but I'm not surprised. Karen said she'd be able to provide security for both Carolyn and the kids, so that part should work out. But I'd like to put an end to this before Carolyn comes back to be a target again."

"Amen to that. By your alternative to Karen's plan?"

"Yep. And I'm going to need your help with it. You game?"

Martin snorted. "To help you get the bitch that's after Carolyn? Bet your ass I want to be part of it."

"Kinda figured that's what you'd say. Okay, first thing I need you to do is to make sure Carolyn doesn't reset her email password."

"Because you don't want to alert the killer that we suspect Carolyn's been hacked?" he asked.

"Exactly. We don't want to do anything to spook her. Tell Carolyn to use her email like she normally would, just not for anything that would reveal your plans or location. We'll use your phone to communicate anything that needs to be kept confidential."

"Okay, got it. And we could also use Carolyn's email for disinformation," he suggested.

I wasn't surprised that Martin pointed that out before I mentioned it. Even without knowing what I was planning, he was quick to realize that misleading the killer could work to our advantage.

"Indeed. And there are two emails in that regard that I want her to send out right away. The first is to her lab personnel, saying that she's going to be out for the next two or three weeks. She can add that she's decided to continue her vacation with the kids and they're going up to Mount Katahdin and the North Maine Woods, however she'd normally write a message like that."

"And the second?"

"An email to me, saying the same thing, but adding that she's uncomfortable coming home after her house was vandalized. And asking if I can manage the clinical trials while she's away."

"Aren't you concerned that'll make the killer think we're suspicious?" Martin asked.

"No. Because I'm going to reply that she should enjoy the trip but doesn't need to worry. Karen's still investigating but feels confident that it was just a random break-in that won't be repeated. As well as saying that I'll be happy to step in and manage the trials."

"Wait a minute," Martin objected. "What if that makes you the target instead of Carolyn?"

"I hope it does. And I'm going to set a trap that I don't think the killer will be able to resist."

I went ahead and told him the rest of what I was thinking. His reaction was just what I expected.

"Are you fucking crazy?! Putting a big juicy target on your back and acting as bait for a lunatic murderer is your idea of a plan?"

"Pretty much. But you'll be there to help me take her down."

"Oh, right. And that's supposed to make it okay? Why the hell are you trying to set this up when Karen's not going to be there? I know I'm good, but having Karen and some of her cops there would be even better."

"Except I'm pretty sure the killer won't come after me if Karen or her guys are around," I explained. "Think about how much trouble she went through to find a time when the kids were away before she made a run at Carolyn. And she probably realizes that Karen's a cop, who already shot at her once. What I want to do is to give her an opening when she knows Karen's out of town and thinks I'm alone and vulnerable. Except it'll be a setup, and we'll be waiting for her. You in?"

"Of course, I'm in, what do you think? I'll have Carolyn send the emails as soon as we disconnect. Then just let me know where and when you need me."

Carolyn's email arrived less than ten minutes later. My cue to bait the trap.

I responded to Carolyn and then sent an email to the same lists of Maine oncologists and MTRI personnel that had received my earlier announcement of the trials. Except I deliberately made a minor misspelling in the address of the Maine oncologist list, so the email only went to the MTRI lists.

Dear colleagues,

I'm writing to let you know of an organizational change in our clinical trials. Carolyn Gelman will be away on personal business for the next two to three weeks, possibly longer. During her absence, I will serve as medical director for both of the trials I wrote to you about earlier.

Until further notice, please contact me with patient referrals or any questions you may have.

Brad Parker, Director, Maine Translational Research Institute

Then I sent off one more email, this time to Karen, confirming a meeting I knew she had scheduled for this coming Friday evening. The last piece of bait that would be waiting for the killer once she got into my email account.

Just checking, are you still going to be in Augusta Friday evening for your meeting with Major Thomas? If so, I'll plan to work late that night too. Need time to catch up on all the clinical trial stuff.

Her response was immediate.

Yes, I won't be home until probably around ten. Glad you can use the time!

Finally, I called security and asked them to install a surveillance camera in my office before the end of the day. If the killer tried to hack my computer by installing a hardware keylogger, we'd get her on video. Alternatively, if she tried a phishing email, I'd be able to spot it because it would come from someone outside the institute.

I was ready. Now it was the killer's turn.

CHAPTER 39

SHIRLEY

She read the emails from Gelman and Parker three times to make sure she wasn't missing anything. Then she decided to go home for the rest of the day to think things through. There was a lot going on, a lot of things that seemed to be changing.

It looked like Gelman sensed that something more than a simple break-in had happened. But despite her fears, neither Parker nor his cop girlfriend seemed to be worried. Or more importantly, had any inkling of what she'd really intended.

At least not yet. But if the cop girlfriend was still investigating, it was always possible she'd come across something that would give the game away. And Gelman being nervous about coming home might be enough to keep her working the case.

With two murders already under her belt, sitting around waiting for Gelman to return from her travels didn't seem like the wisest choice. Maybe it would be smart to cut and run. Fake identification papers and an ample supply of cash were all ready to go. She could get in the car now and be in Canada tonight. Nobody would miss her, not really. And after a little time passed, she could start a new life and carry on her work. Someplace where her discoveries could immediately be used to benefit the people who needed them, without the need to sacrifice others as "controls."

But she wasn't ready yet. Vengeance demanded more deaths, and she wasn't about to stop until justice was done.

She'd enjoyed making Salton pay. It had been incredibly satisfying, better than science, sex, or anything else she'd experienced. And then Lowell had presented himself. Another callous piece of crap who felt justified in killing patients who trusted him by using them as controls. Her knife had longed for his blood, and she'd reveled in quenching its thirst.

And then Gelman rose up as the next Lowell. But despite her careful planning, things had gone wrong. Nonetheless, it was only by dumb luck that Parker and his girlfriend had shown up, and she wasn't going to let that stop her. Her mission wasn't finished.

But maybe her next victim shouldn't be Gelman. Parker had decided to assume Gelman's role as medical director, so let him take her place as the third victim as well. After all, he was Gelman's boss. And he was the one who was initially going to recruit Salton and then brought in Lowell. He was the man in charge, the director of the medical directors. Killing him would be a fitting culmination to her efforts.

She'd just have to get him when his cop girlfriend wasn't around. After the way the bitch pulled a gun without hesitation on Saturday, Shirley knew she couldn't deal with her. But there had to be times when they were separated, when she could catch Parker alone.

It was the same problem she'd faced finding a time to get Gelman, and she decided to solve it the same way. Except physical access to Parker's computer would be tricky. It was in the director's office suite, so she couldn't just sneak into his office to install a hardware keylogger. This time she'd have to use a phishing email.

It would be simple to add a software keylogger to a fake patient's record and send it to Parker in response to his email. She'd just have to make it look like it was from a practicing oncologist, since he'd probably do an internet search to check out the sender. It would be easy enough for her to use a real physician's name, but what if he went a step further and tried to verify the sender's identity by phone?

It took a minute, but then the answer hit her. *It was summer.* People went on vacations, so she just had to find an oncologist who was away and use their name to respond to Parker.

She started with a search for oncologists in Bangor, figuring that was far enough from Wells that Parker probably wouldn't know people there. That yielded a list of more than forty physicians, with the locations and phone numbers of their offices.

She called the first number on the list and asked if she could speak to Dr. Jameson. "This is Janet Thompson from the Maine Board of Licensure in Medicine," she explained. "I need to clarify an issue that's been raised about the doctor's license renewal." When the obviously flustered receptionist asked her to wait while she got Dr. Jameson, Shirley hung up.

A more or less similar exchange followed Shirley's calls to the next eight offices, but then she struck paydirt. Dr. Blackfin was away on vacation for the next two weeks. Shirley reassured the receptionist that there was no immediate problem, and she'd call back after he returned.

Then she had another thought. Since Dr. Blackfin was going to be unavailable, it would make sense for him to suggest that Parker contact the patient directly. If he did, that might give her a chance to set up a private appointment with him. An appointment that would be his last.

Turning to her computer, she set up two new Gmail accounts under the names of Dr. Robert Blackfin and Shirley Leavitt. Why not? There was no reason not to use Shirley for the name of Blackfin's supposed patient. Then she used the Blackfin account to respond to Parker's email.

Dear Dr. Parker,

I'm an oncologist in Bangor, and I'm treating a patient who I think would be a good candidate for one of your clinical trials. As you can see from the attached record, Shirley Leavitt is a thirty-four-year-old female with advanced lung cancer that has failed to respond to radiation and carboplatin.

I'm away on vacation for the next two weeks and will have only sporadic access to email while camping in the North Woods. I'll be happy to speak with you when I return, but feel free to reach out to the patient directly (sleavitt@gmail.com) if you wish to set up an appointment with her in my absence. I've already told her about your trial, and she is quite interested in being a participant.

Sincerely,

Robert Blackfin, MD

She'd downloaded software when she purchased the hardware keylogger, so she concocted a medical record for Shirley Leavitt, added the keylogger software, and attached the package to her email. All Parker had to do was open the attachment, and she'd have his password.

She sat back and waited for the keylogger to come to life.

CHAPTER 40
BRAD

I almost jumped out of my chair when I saw the email from Dr. Robert Blackfin. *This is it!* Out of curiosity, I searched for Robert Blackfin and found that he was indeed an oncologist in Bangor. Then I called his office number and was told that Dr. Blackfin was away on vacation, just like the phishing email had said. The killer must have called a bunch of doctors' offices to find one who was out of town. A lot of work to be sure that I'd accept the email as legitimate.

Not giving me an opportunity for further contact with Dr. Blackfin made sense, but why had the killer suggested that I contact the patient? Could she be hoping it would give her the chance to arrange a private appointment with me? If that was it, I'd be happy to oblige. And turn the trap she was planning for me into my trap for her.

I opened the attachment and glanced at the patient's history, which looked plausible enough. Then I logged out of my email, waited a few minutes, and logged back in, so that a keylogger could record my password for the killer. Then I forced myself to wait an hour to allow the killer time to search through my emails and realize that Friday evening would give her an opportunity to catch me alone.

When I thought it had been long enough, I sent an email to Shirley Leavitt.

Dear Ms. Leavitt,

I've received a message from Dr. Blackfin, referring you as a potential participant in one of the clinical trials we have underway at MTRI. After reviewing your history, I think you meet the criteria for participation and could indeed benefit from one of our new drugs.

As the next step, I would like to meet with you to discuss the clinical trial process, including the potential risks and benefits. I am scheduling these appointments for one hour time slots, preferably in the early evenings to fit them in with my other responsibilities. However, if that's not convenient, I'll find time to see you during the regular workday.

Please let me know if you'd like to arrange a meeting, ideally in the next few days so we can get your treatment started as soon as possible.

Sincerely,

Dr. Brad Parker, Clinical Trial Director, MTRI

The next step was key. Would she come back with a request to meet Friday evening? The institute would be largely empty by six on a Friday, and with Karen away, I hoped Shirley would seize it as an ideal opportunity. I paced the office as I waited nervously. But before too long, she responded.

Dear Dr. Parker,

Thank you for your encouraging message. I would very much like to meet, and since I am still working, an evening appointment would be perfect.

Is there any chance that this Friday would work? I can get off a little early on Fridays, so I could make it to your office from Bangor by seven.

Thank you so much for giving me this opportunity.

Shirley Leavitt

My first thought was, *Gotcha!*

Followed by, *Congratulations, Brad. You just made a date with a murderer who's planning to make you her next victim.*

CHAPTER 41

SHIRLEY

She could hardly believe it when Parker responded to her email.

Friday at seven is fine. My office is in the director's suite on the first floor of MTRI, and I'll leave the door unlocked. I look forward to seeing you.

It had been so easy. He'd be alone in his office, with his cop girlfriend ninety miles away in Augusta. The only problem was that killing him at MTRI would focus attention on the people who worked there, and she wouldn't have a plausible alibi. But it didn't matter. Parker's death would be the grand finale of her mission, and she'd be prepared to take off for Canada as soon as it was done. With any luck, she'd be hours away before his body was discovered.

It wasn't until later that caution set in. *Had it been* too *easy?* Could she be walking into a trap that Parker and his cop girlfriend had set? What if her trip to Augusta was a ruse, and she'd be waiting in Parker's office Friday evening, maybe with some of her fellow cops? Ready to make an arrest. *Or to just shoot me.*

She went to the kitchen and poured a larger-than-usual glass of wine. She needed to calm down and think this through. The two picnic tables in the grassy common area in back of her apartment building were unoccupied, so she took her wine outside, seizing the opportunity to escape the confines of her tiny efficiency. It was all she could afford on her meager salary, and she didn't want to waste her reserve cash on everyday needs. But she looked forward to leaving it behind when her mission was finished.

But would it be safe to make that Friday evening? She decided the best way to approach that question was to think through what Parker and his girlfriend would have needed to know in order to make this a setup. Gelman's email had said that she was uncomfortable about coming home after what happened Saturday, so she must be suspicious that it was more than a random break-in. If so, girlfriend's cop brain might think it had been planned for a time when Gelman and her kids were out of the house. And guessed that the burglar had hacked into Gelman's computer to find such a time. If they got that far, it would be a logical next step to think that, if she were after Parker, she'd hack into *his* computer to find a time when *he'd* be alone. And then they might have planted a fake email leading her to think that girlfriend would be away Friday evening.

Maybe that was possible, Shirley conceded, *but it seemed like an awful lot for them to have put together.* For one thing, why would they have assumed that someone who was after Gelman would change targets and go after Parker? Just because Gelman and Parker were colleagues didn't seem like a good reason. And even if they had made that unlikely jump, how would they have known to bait the trap using Parker's mailing list for the clinical trial announcements? Or that she'd pose as a patient in response? There was nothing connecting that mailing list to the Gelman break-in. Nor was there anything connecting the break-in to clinical trials in general, or to the Salton and Lowell murders in particular.

Putting it all together, she didn't think she'd be walking into a trap Friday. It should be safe to proceed, although she'd be even more careful than usual. Starting by verifying that the girlfriend's trip to Augusta was for real.

Step one was to figure out who Parker's girlfriend was. Her first initial and last name were given in the address of Parker's email to her, so it wasn't hard to search the internet and find that she was a lieutenant in the Maine State Police and commanding officer of a major crimes unit, MCU-South. *Impressive*, Shirley thought. *Definitely not someone I want to tangle with.*

Next, she searched for Major Thomas, with whom Richmond was supposedly meeting Friday evening in Augusta. It didn't take long to establish that Thomas was the operations major in charge of the state police patrol troops and major crimes units. That would mean Thomas was Richmond's boss, so it was reasonable that she'd be meeting with him at his office in Augusta. So far, so good.

It was after six o'clock, but she thought the state police might work late, so she called the number provided for Thomas on the website. When a woman answered, she introduced herself as Lieutenant Richmond's staff assistant at MCU-South.

"I'm sorry to trouble you, but we're having some confusion about Lieutenant Richmond's schedule. Is she meeting with Major Thomas in Augusta on Friday?"

"No bother, let me just check. Yes, here it is. Right, the major has a meeting with Lieutenant Richmond and the other commanding officers who report to him at six Friday evening. We're having a light dinner brought in, and it'll probably run until eight or so."

Shirley thanked the woman and smiled. Richmond would be away as planned Friday evening. She'd still be careful, but there was no reason not to proceed.

CHAPTER 42

BRAD

decided not to call Martin until I got home. It seemed highly unlikely that Shirley could have bugged my office, but why take the chance? I left a bit earlier than usual, stopped to pick up a prepaid cell phone at Walgreens, and was home nearly an hour before I expected Karen. Rosie was thrilled to see me, so I gave her dinner and took her down to the beach, where she could play in the waves and pretend to chase the sandpipers while I brought Martin up to date.

He took me by surprise when he answered the phone with a curt "Dawson," rather than his usual jovial greeting. Then I realized that he wouldn't have recognized my burner phone's number.

"Hi Martin, it's me. I'm calling from a burner."

"Well, that explains why I didn't know who was calling. But why a burner?"

"Our killer took the bait and hacked my computer, so I figured she might've gotten into my phone too," I explained. "I'm probably being paranoid, but better safe than sorry."

He chuckled. "No question that you're paranoid. But you're also right about excessive caution not hurting. Especially given who you're dealing with. How far did you get with her?"

"All the way. I have an appointment with her scheduled for Friday evening at seven."

"Huh! Fast work! Okay, I'll make up some excuse for Carolyn and be ready to come down and join the party. But listen—"

Before Martin could finish the sentence, we were interrupted by the loud squawking of half a dozen seagulls Rosie had decided to torment. She might be getting older and a little slower, but she was still full of piss and vinegar.

When the noise quieted down a bit, Martin asked, "What the hell's going on?"

"Just some seagulls. Protesting because Rosie's chasing them."

"Seagulls, huh? Well, I know you like birds, so I guess that makes some sort of sense. Anyway, what I started to say was, I think it's time for you to let Karen in on this. I'm sure she'll want to cancel her trip to Augusta and be there with us to take this crazy bitch down. She could bring a couple of guys along and be all set to haul our friend's ass off to jail as soon as she shows up at your office."

I stifled a sigh. Didn't Martin realize how much I'd fussed and fretted about this? "I don't doubt that's how she'd want to play it. And she'll be royally pissed when she finds out what I'm planning instead. But I'm afraid that if she doesn't go to Augusta, it'll tip off the killer. Who's calling herself Shirley, by the way."

"Shirley, is it? How nice. But as long as you don't put anything in email, how would Shirley know if Karen changed her plans?"

"It's just too chancy. Whoever Shirley is, she's smart enough to have committed two murders without getting caught. And it would have been three, if Karen and I hadn't suddenly decided to surprise Carolyn on her birthday. She could follow Karen to Augusta, stick a tracker under her car, call Augusta to be sure Karen's there . . . the list could go on and on. And if she gets scared and bolts, we'll never get her."

"All right, I hear you. So how about Karen going up north as a decoy, but arranging for a couple of cops to join us at MTRI?"

"Again, too risky. I'm worried about them being spotted. There won't be many people around the institute that late on a Friday, and anyone who doesn't belong will stick out like a sore thumb."

"And our friend Shirley will probably be on high alert," Martin acknowledged. "Okay, I can see that. But then how about me? I'm not part of your institute either."

"No, but we can set up cover for you as a visiting seminar speaker. I'm thinking you get to MTRI around two, and I'll give you a tour so people will get a look at you. Then you give an institute-wide seminar at the end of the day, which I'll advertise as a big deal and lay on a wine and cheese reception afterward. When that's done, I'll go back to my office, and you can wait in the lobby, theoretically until I'm ready for us to go out to dinner."

"And I take it there's someplace I can hang out where I'll be positioned to grab Shirley when she shows up?"

"Mm-hmm. There's a seating area with a good view of both the main entrance and the door to my director's suite."

He finally capitulated. "All right, I get it. I'll have the Glock Karen gave me Saturday. I assume you'll be armed, too?"

"For sure. I'll just borrow one of the guns Karen has at home."

"And all Shirley has is a knife?"

"As far as we know. That's what she used on Salton and Lowell. And if she carried a gun, I think she'd have returned fire when Karen shot at her Saturday."

"Okay, that makes sense," he said. "And you know what they say about bringing a knife to a gunfight."

"Exactly. The two of us shouldn't have any problem taking her down. And then we can give the cops a call."

Just as we ended the call, Rosie started barking and ran toward the house. When I turned to see what was going on, I spotted Karen coming down to the beach. I felt my usual excitement at seeing her, but this time it was tinged with regret.

I'd never lied to her or misled her before, and I didn't like the way it felt now.

CHAPTER 43

SHIRLEY

She got up early Friday morning, having spent a restless night worrying about all the things that could go wrong today. But in the end, she was confident that she could pull it off. Once she got Parker alone in his office, he'd be no harder to handle than Salton or Lowell had been. None of the administrative staff would still be in the director's suite at seven on a Friday evening, so as long as Richmond or her cops didn't show up, it should all go as planned.

She'd leave directly from MTRI as soon as the deed was done, so she loaded up her Mitsubishi SUV with the limited amount of stuff she wanted to take to Canada. Pictures of her mother, her stash of cash, her fake passport and driver's license, and a few clothes. And, of course, the tote bag with her laptop, her knife, some zip tie handcuffs, and a Taser.

She hadn't needed the handcuffs or Taser for Salton or Lowell. It had been easier to move fast and just use her knife. But she thought it might be interesting to take a little more time with Parker and explain what was happening before she finished him off. And for that, incapacitating him with the Taser and restraining him with the handcuffs would be necessary.

She made a last check of her apartment to make sure she wasn't forgetting anything. But she didn't have anything worth worrying about anyway, so she went out to her car and drove off without giving the shithole a second look.

The MTRI parking lot was only about one-third full when she got there, but she took a few minutes to study the cars that were there. As she hoped, there wasn't anything odd that might signal the presence of cops waiting to arrest her. It was still early, of course, but she'd repeat the process at intervals throughout the day.

Satisfied for now, she took her tote bag, went into the institute, and proceeded to her lab. Time to start another day at work.

CHAPTER 44

BRAD

Karen was still in bed when I gave up on sleep and took Rosie down to the kitchen to make coffee. I'd spent a restless night, alternately fretting about what could happen if things went wrong and how Karen would react when it was all over. Despite the danger, I was more worried about Karen than I was about Shirley. Partly because I was confident that Martin and I wouldn't have much of a problem handling her. But more because I was breaking the bond of trust that had always been at the foundation of my relationship with Karen.

Once Karen came downstairs, she filled a mug with coffee, came out to the deck to sit next to me, and asked, "What's wrong? You were tossing and turning all night, and this morning you look like crap."

I tried to laugh it off. "Gee, thanks. Sorry I don't look knockout gorgeous like you first thing in the morning."

She wasn't having any of it. "Bullshit. Something's bothering you. Are you going to tell me what's going on, or do I have to drag it out of you?"

I sighed. She'd always been able to read me. But at least I

should be able to put her off until tonight, when I'd be able to explain. *Or try to.*

"Okay, you're right. There's a serious problem at the institute that I'm going to have to deal with today, and I guess it's been weighing on me. But it's complicated, and there's not enough time to talk it through before we have to go to work. How about waiting until tonight, and then I'll tell you all about it?"

She gave me a long questioning look before finally shrugging her shoulders. "All right, if you think that's better. You remember I have that dinner meeting in Augusta tonight? But I should be home by ten."

"I remember. We can talk when you get home, if it's not too late. Otherwise, I'll fill you in tomorrow morning."

She let it go, and we made small talk while we finished our coffee and got ready for work. When we were leaving, we exchanged our usual kiss goodbye, but then she held me tightly instead of letting go. "Good luck with whatever you're facing today, Professor. I love you."

"And I love you, Lieutenant," I replied.

As I watched her get into her car, I wondered how much guiltier I'd feel if I were planning to cheat on her this afternoon. Or maybe then I wouldn't care so much, and this felt worse.

After Karen left, I selected a Glock 17 from her collection and drove to the institute. I needed to watch myself today. Whoever Shirley was, I was sure she'd be alert to any sign that I might be suspicious. I needed to follow my normal routine until this afternoon when Martin arrived and then transition into my standard mode of hosting a visiting scientist. Shirley's antennae would be up, and I couldn't afford to do anything out of the ordinary.

I started off the morning, as usual, in the director's office, where Anna greeted me with coffee, a half dozen memos requiring my signature, and a reminder that I had a ten o'clock meeting with our director of core facilities, Ed Philipson. I took it all into my office where the first thing I did was put the gun I'd borrowed from

Karen in a desk drawer. It would be safe there during the day, and easy for me to grab when Shirley came in at seven. Unless Martin stopped her first.

Then I checked my email and, having found nothing important, turned to the memos Anna had given me. None of them required much in the way of concentration, which was fortunate since my mind was still busy switching back and forth between what would happen during Shirley's visit and what I'd say to Karen afterward.

Ed Philipson showed up promptly at ten with his laptop so that we could review his monthly summary of the core facility's budget. I got up from my desk, and we sat at my conference table to go over the data, which I liked to keep an eye on since the core equipment was such a critical part of the institute. As usual, Ed had it all well in hand, and the operating costs were balanced either by fees charged to the users' research grants or by funds budgeted in the institute's core grant. When we finished going over his spreadsheet, I asked if he'd be available this afternoon to give a visitor a tour of the facility.

He looked surprised at my request. "Of course, but that's not usually something you ask me to do. You generally like to show visitors around yourself."

I smiled faintly. "True. But today's visitor is an old friend who used to be a dean at Yale, and I think he'd be interested in getting into the weeds of how you run the place. Maybe you can take him around, introduce him to some of your staff, and explain how you handle the finances for the major instruments. If you have the time, of course."

Ed bowed his head and said he'd be honored. I was sure he'd make enough of a production of Martin's visit that the technical staff in his facility, who probably wouldn't come to the seminar, would have a chance to see who he was. Just in case Shirley was one of Ed's techs.

For the same reason, I called Stan Jacobs and asked if he could give Martin a tour of our clinical facility. Like Ed, Stan was surprised at the request but happily agreed when I explained that Martin was a former dean who would be interested in how the clinic was funded, as well as in how the institute's clinical work interfaced with our basic research programs. The latter was a particular point of pride for Stan, and I was confident he'd give Martin a tour that would let him be seen by the clinical staff.

Seminar notices, which prominently displayed Martin's photograph, had already been posted throughout the institute, and most of the institute's students and scientists would be at Martin's talk. Not to mention the wine and cheese reception afterward. By the end of the day, Shirley would have had ample opportunity to learn who Martin was. And presumably wouldn't be alarmed if she saw him waiting for me in the lobby.

After talking to Ed and Stan, I felt like my head was starting to function again. Martin still wouldn't be here for a couple of hours, so I finished the morning's administrative chores and went to my lab to check in with my students. For most of them, a quick visit was all I needed to confirm that their experiments were proceeding normally. One of the graduate students, Pam, however, was bogged down with a technical problem that I thought I might be able to help with. We sat down and went through her protocols in detail until finally, nearly forty-five minutes later, I could see what the problem was. Once I explained it, Pam saw it too, and I left feeling good about having done something useful.

Ginger greeted me with her usual enthusiasm when I got to her bench in the back. "I just got some neat results with a new double-antibody ADC. It uses the same antibodies, but they're conjugated to a different drug. Want to see?"

"Of course. When am I not interested in new results?"

She smiled and opened her notebook. "I set up the experiment to compare the new double-antibody ADC with our current one, the one about to go into the clinical trial. I've just analyzed the data for five cell lines so far, but you can see they all respond better to the new one."

I looked at the data. "Hmm, interesting. These aren't big differences, but you're right. Your new drug looks significantly better against all five of these cell lines. Nice work!"

"Thanks, I thought you'd be pleased. I still have data on another half dozen lines to work up. If they look good too, I'll get started on some tumor explants."

I gave her a thumbs-up. "Great. By the time we get the trial started, you'll have a new and better version ready to go."

She was smiling when I left, thinking that she truly was amazing. She really didn't need me anymore, not like Pam and my other students did. I was happy to provide Ginger with an appreciative ear, but she was ready to strike out on her own in an independent faculty position. Nothing made me feel better than watching a student reach this point, when I knew I'd helped launch someone on the road to making new discoveries of their own.

On that high note, I went back to my office. Martin would be here soon.

CHAPTER 45

Martin burst into my office a few minutes before two o'clock, followed by a very flustered Anna. "I'm so sorry, he just pushed right past me!"

"No worries," I assured her. "He's been like that all the years I've known him." I got up and pumped Martin's hand. "How you doing, buddy? All set for later?"

I might have been asking if he was ready to give his upcoming lecture, but we both knew that wasn't the "later" I was referring to.

"All set." He gave me a penetrating look. "Are you?"

"Yep, I'm good to go. We have some time before your talk, so let me show you around the institute."

I led the way across the lobby to Stan Jacobs's office in the clinic, past a large poster advertising Martin's seminar.

"You seem to have quite a few of these plastered around," he commented. "With my picture and everything. Do you always promote seminars this aggressively?"

"Not really, but I wanted everyone to get a good look at your ugly mug."

He nodded approvingly. "So they'll recognize me if they see me waiting for you in the lobby later?"

"Mm-hmm. Which is also why I've asked Stan Jacobs to give you a tour of our clinical facilities. Most of the clinical staff probably won't come to your talk, so this'll give them a chance to get a look at you."

Martin sighed. "Sounds boring as hell, but I see your point. Let's get it over with."

Stan was as thorough and methodical as I expected. And as boring as Martin feared. When it was over and we were alone again, Martin drew a long, loud breath. "Thank God that's finally done. I hope you have something more interesting planned next."

"Don't worry, you'll have plenty of excitement before the day's finished. But for now, our core facilities director is waiting to give you a tour. I told him you were a former dean, so he's planning on explaining how he handles the budget."

Martin groaned. "I'm sure that'll be fascinating. But I assume this is another ruse to show my face to a group of people who won't come to the seminar?"

I said he was right, and he reluctantly followed me to Ed Philipson's office.

Happily, Ed turned out to be a more engaging host than Stan had been, and I was surprised when Martin actually seemed interested in the financial model. He didn't usually display polite tolerance for something he disliked, so I wasn't surprised when he commented afterward that he'd been impressed.

"You've not only assembled an up-to-date collection of major instruments, but it sounds like the fee structure you've established makes it easy for your faculty to give something new a try. Quite a nice setup."

"Thanks, I appreciate that. I've tried to work the budget out so that the operational costs of each item of major equipment are covered from charges to its principal users. That way, a faculty member who just needs to run a pilot experiment can do so for a nominal fee. They only start paying their full share if an instrument does what they need and they start using it regularly."

"And from the way your guy Ed described it, the system seems to work well. I can see why I had such a hard time trying to steal Carolyn last year."

I gave him a wink. "You might not have gotten her to move to Yale, but it seems like you recruited her quite successfully on a personal level. Or vice versa."

He grinned. "Yeah, things are good between us. Pretty soon we may even have to tackle the living-in-separate-cities problem. But first, and speaking of Carolyn, she said I should get you to introduce me to the postdoc who developed your new drug. According to Carolyn, she's quite impressive."

"Ginger? Carolyn's right, she's a star. We still have nearly half an hour before your seminar, let's go see if she's in the lab."

Ginger was at her desk, seemingly immersed in a spreadsheet. When I interrupted her, she looked up with her usual smile. "This is the experiment with the additional cell lines that I told you about this morning. I'm still putting the data together, but it's looking good. Maybe I can show you later if you have time?"

"Sounds great, although it might have to wait until tomorrow. The seminar's less than half an hour from now, and I'm going to be tied up after that. But I wanted to introduce you to the speaker, an old friend of mine. Martin Dawson."

Turning to Martin, she gushed, "Oh, Dr. Dawson! I'm so happy to meet you. I really enjoyed your recent paper in *Cell Biology*. Will you be talking about that this afternoon?"

Martin looked pleased. "I will be, thank you. And there are a few new twists to the story that you might be interested in. But first, Carolyn Gelman told me that your work with Brad was really impressive. I'd love it if you had a few minutes to tell me about it."

"Of course, but do we have time before your talk?"

Martin shrugged. "All I have to do is plug in my laptop."

"And the lecture hall is only two minutes away," I added. "Go ahead, Ginger, you're good for the next twenty minutes."

I felt a little bad, asking her to give a command performance with no advance warning. But I figured Ginger could handle it, and she did. Without any hesitation, she took Martin through the published experiments that established the effectiveness of double-compared to single-antibody ADCs. Then she showed him the data with additional tumor explants that she'd obtained since we submitted the paper and concluded with the newest data she'd shown me this morning.

Martin was visibly impressed. "That's a beautiful story, Ginger. All I can say is, congratulations on a piece of work that's not only impressive science, but also is very soon going to be helping patients who need it."

Ginger was grinning from ear to ear, and Martin would have gone on, but it was almost time for his seminar.

"C'mon Martin, we need to get going," I interrupted. "Ginger, that was a great presentation, thank you. Are you coming to the lecture?"

"Of course, I'll be there in a minute. You go ahead; I just need to put my stuff away first."

On the way to the seminar, I asked Martin if he'd spotted a killer on our tours.

"Just your clinical director trying to bore us to death. But I have to say, Ginger seems terrific. You're lucky to have her."

I didn't disagree with either conclusion.

CHAPTER 46

I t was two minutes after four o'clock when we got to the auditorium. The room was already packed, so I went to the podium to start my introduction while Martin set up his computer. Looking out at the audience, I couldn't help wondering if one of them was a murderer who was planning to kill me a few hours from now. Could Shirley be someone I knew, maybe even thought of as a friend? Possible, perhaps, but it seemed more likely that she was one of the many staff and students at MTRI that I'd never met.

I pushed those speculations to the back of my mind and proceeded to give a brief summary of Martin's academic history and research accomplishments. I added that he'd been a dean of Yale Medical School until a year ago when he realized he was too smart to be an administrator and had gone back to the lab full time. Then I asked the audience to welcome Martin to tell us about some of the fruits of his return to research.

Martin strode to the podium amid a welcoming round of applause. He thanked me for the introduction and charmed the audience by adding that it was a pleasure to visit MTRI and "see that good science doesn't require the cutthroat atmosphere of New Haven but can flourish in a pleasant and collegial place in Maine." Then he went ahead to give an eloquent seminar as if he didn't have a care in the world. No hint that he was visiting our "pleasant and collegial place" to catch a killer.

Martin's talk was well received, with loud applause followed by a lengthy series of questions from the audience. When I finally ended the session and invited everyone to join us for wine and cheese, it was after five thirty. Anna had set up tables with assorted cheeses, wine, and soft drinks in a room just off the main lobby, and most of the audience migrated there to have a glass of wine before heading home. Quite a few lingered to chat or to come up to Martin with questions, congratulations on his work, or just thanks for visiting. It was a Friday afternoon, though, and the last of the stragglers was gone by six thirty.

A few minutes later, Martin and I left the reception room to find an empty lobby. The time for the real business of the day had finally come.

I led Martin to a lounge-like seating area, with leather armchairs and a couch arranged around a coffee table. "I think this is the best place for you to wait. It's out of the main traffic pattern, but you're just a few steps from the entrance to the director's suite. And you'll see anybody heading for the door, whether they're coming in from the main entrance, down the stairs or elevator from a research floor, or through the hall from the clinic."

Martin looked skeptical. "Why don't I just station myself inside the suite? That way, I'll be able to grab our friend Shirley as soon as she comes in."

"There isn't really any place to sit inside. Besides my office, there's just Anna's desk in the front room and a few visitor chairs."

"That's all right. I could sit at the front desk and be ready for her."

I rolled my eyes. "Right, you look just like my administrative assistant. That'd fool her for sure."

Martin looked puzzled for a moment, but then he got it. "Sorry, I forgot for a minute that our friend Shirley probably knows your admin. As well as who I am by now."

"Exactly. And if you were a distinguished visitor who needed to hang out for an hour before we went to dinner, this lounge area is where I'd put you. It's comfortable, you can plug your laptop in if you need to, and you can even snag some more wine from the reception if you're so inclined."

"And I'll be able to see Shirley coming and follow her into the office," Martin added. "Okay, you're right. And where'll you be?"

"Sitting at my desk. I told her that I'd leave the entrance to the suite unlocked, and I'm going to leave my office door open, so I'll know when she comes in. And I'll have my gun handy."

CHAPTER 47

SHIRLEY

She skipped the reception and went back to the lab when the seminar was finished. It was time for final preparations. Including safety checks—a last chance to make sure she wasn't about to walk into a trap.

Her first call was to MCU-South, Richmond's major crimes unit. When she said she needed to speak to Lieutenant Richmond, the officer who answered said that the lieutenant wasn't available and asked if he could help her.

"Thank you, but she wanted me to talk to her directly about this," Shirley responded. "Is there a time when I could reach her later?"

"I'm sorry, she's left for the day to go to a meeting in Augusta. She'll be in first thing tomorrow morning, if you'd like to leave a message."

Shirley thanked him and said she'd call in the morning. So far, so good.

Her next call was to Major Thomas's office at state police headquarters in Augusta. "I'm trying to reach Lieutenant Karen Richmond from MCU-South. I believe she's there for a meeting with Major Thomas and wonder if I could speak to her?"

"Yes ma'am, she's attending the commanding officers' dinner meeting with the major. It won't be starting for a few more minutes; do you want me to see if I can find her?"

"No, that's all right. I can wait and catch her tomorrow."

She ended the call satisfied. Richmond was safely out of the way in Augusta. All clear to go ahead.

Next, she got ready to leave the lab for the last time. She gathered up her lab notebooks and put them in the tote bag with her laptop, knife, zip ties, and Taser. Looking around the room, she realized that was all she needed. Her notebooks, together with the protocols and spreadsheets on her computer, had all the information necessary to reproduce her work, so once she got set up in a new lab, there'd be no problem continuing her research. Someplace where it could be used to help people who needed it without having to sacrifice innocent "controls."

Shouldering the now overloaded tote bag, she went out to her car. The reception was emptying out, and she was one of many leaving the institute for the weekend. Parker and his friend Dawson were busy talking to a couple of stragglers, so they didn't seem to notice her.

Once she got the notebooks unloaded and boxed up in her trunk, she surveyed the cars parked in the lot. Most of the vehicles that had been there before were gone by now, and she recognized those that remained from earlier in the day. Except for a silver BMW parked toward the back.

A chill ran down her spine. Could that belong to Richmond's detectives? She strolled over to it nonchalantly, pretending to be watching a hawk perched in a tree at the edge of the lot. And then she saw it bore Connecticut plates. *Of course, it belongs to Parker's friend from Yale,* she realized. Not a problem.

But then another thought struck her. If Dawson was still here, where was he? Would she have to deal with him as well as Parker?

Her questions were answered as soon as she went back inside. Parker was on his way into the director's suite, where she was going to meet him in just under half an hour. Dawson wasn't with him, which looked promising. But then she spotted Dawson in the lobby lounge. He had his laptop out and was presumably going to wait there until her meeting with Parker was finished.

Unless he was standing guard. But that didn't seem likely. If Parker suspected something was wrong, he'd have brought in Richmond and her cops, not just another professor. But either way, she couldn't very well leave Dawson sitting outside the office. He'd have to be neutralized.

She didn't want to kill him, though, so she hurried back to her lab, where she had a vial of propofol, a common surgical anesthetic. She'd stolen it from the clinic back in April, but like her Taser, she hadn't needed it to deal with Salton or Lowell. Now its time had come. She filled a syringe with enough to knock Dawson out and returned to the lobby, where he was still sitting in the lounge area.

She gave him a friendly wave and went over to him. "That was really a great seminar! Most of the work we do here is focused pretty directly on treatment, like development of new drugs. It was fun hearing about research that's pure basic science for a change."

He smiled. "Thank you, I'm glad you enjoyed it."

"There is one thing I wanted to ask you about, though. Let me just check my notes."

She reached into her tote bag and pulled out her Taser. His eyes bulged and his mouth flopped open in shock, but it was too late. She fired a burst of energy sufficient to immobilize him for thirty seconds. Long enough for her to inject a dose of anesthetic that would keep him out for the next half hour.

When the anesthetic had taken effect, she arranged him on the lounge chair as if he'd fallen asleep. But as she was adjusting his position, her hand brushed against a gun holstered under his jacket. Now it was her turn to be shocked. *Dawson wasn't just a visiting scientist.* He was part of a trap Parker had set to catch her.

She felt a momentary impulse to run, to escape while she still could. But then she forced herself to stop and consider the situation. Through a combination of caution and luck, she'd neutralized Dawson and evaded the trap. Parker would probably be armed too, waiting for her in his office, where she assumed that he and Dawson had planned to capture her. But Parker still didn't know who she was. Now that he no longer had Dawson as backup, there was no reason she couldn't take him by surprise and finish the job.

She added Dawson's gun to her tote bag. Then she turned and walked casually to the director's suite.

CHAPTER 48

BRAD

tensed when I heard the door to the suite open. Shirley wasn't due for another ten minutes. Had she come early? And where was Martin?

I couldn't see who had come in from behind my desk, so I had to be prepared if she'd somehow gotten around Martin. I took my gun out of the drawer and laid it on top of the desk. If Shirley was here, I'd be ready.

Then I heard a familiar voice, and Ginger knocked on my office door. "Brad, I got my new data all organized. Can I show you? It's really neat."

I relaxed and smiled. She never stopped. "I'd love to see it, but I'm waiting for a seven o'clock appointment to show up. A prospective patient for our clinical trial, actually."

She glanced at her watch and shrugged. "You still have ten minutes, and this won't take nearly that long." She took a laptop out of a tote bag and started to open it on my conference table. "Come sit over here. Just two minutes, I promise."

"All right, two minutes." I went over to sit with her at the conference table. "Let's see how quickly you can show me your newest."

She gave me a sardonic grin. "Don't worry, we really don't have to rush. You see, your next appointment is already here." She thrust her hand into the tote bag and came out with a Taser. "*I'm Shirley.*"

My heart started pounding and my arms wouldn't move. "Y . . . y . . . you?" I stammered.

She laughed. But it wasn't the lighthearted laugh I was used to hearing from her. This was more of a cackle, mocking and cruel. "Stupid fool, you never suspected me. It couldn't be your postdoc who worked so hard and always had nice data to show you. Even now, when you knew who would be coming, you came over here to talk to me. Where's your gun, back at your desk? Idiot."

Without further preamble, she fired the Taser. Every muscle in my body clenched up, and I was unable to move. It only lasted a few seconds, but long enough for her to pull zip ties out of her bag and secure my arms and legs to the chair.

When she was satisfied, she reached into her bag again and came out with a large hunting knife. I recognized the serrated blade as she waved it in front of my face.

"You'll recover from the shock soon, and we have some time before I need to kill you. Shall we talk for a bit?"

I'd faced death by violence before, but this was different. My previous encounters had been with would-be assassins driven by motives that I could understand—money, power, or ambition. Trying to deal with a homicidal maniac was something else. Yet, if I hoped to survive, I somehow had to get beyond the paralyzing terror that gripped me and reclaim control.

The only thing I could think of doing was talking to her as if she were sane and hope that I could coax the woman I knew as Ginger to emerge over Shirley. It was probably a vain hope, but talking to her rationally was the only chance I thought I had.

"What'd you do to Martin?" I asked first.

"I gave him a shot of propofol to knock him out. He'll be fine when he wakes up. But don't you want to know why I'm going to kill you?"

"I think I already know why. You told me during your job interview that you'd been touched by cancer firsthand. Did you lose a family member who was a patient of Eric Salton's?" Her eyes widened and she nodded. *I got it right.*

"Were they in one of his clinical trials?" I continued. "And you blamed him for their death because they didn't get the best treatment?"

Her mouth set in a hard line. "The bastard killed my mother. He assigned her to the control group of his big trial of melistomab. She only volunteered for his fucking trial because the drug's phase two results had been incredibly promising. It was obvious that melistomab was far better than anything they already had; Salton didn't need a phase three control group to prove it. She trusted him to treat her cancer, but instead, he condemned her to death just because that's how things were done. So he could win awards like the one he got in Boston."

"That was the night you took your revenge. And then what happened? You decided that other directors of clinical trials deserved the same fate?"

"If they're willfully depriving some patients of the best treatment, they're murderers!" she snarled. "And they deserve to die."

I kept my voice steady, trying to maintain calm. "You chose Steve Lowell as your next victim after I brought him to MTRI to talk to us, right? Just because he was another big name in the clinical trial arena?"

Her grip on the knife tightened. "And because when we met with him, he tried to justify control groups. Even when Penny pressed him on how awful that was. He was no better than another Salton!"

I wasn't sure my strategy was working. It felt like I was talking to Shirley, not to Ginger. A lunatic whose actions made sense in her own world, but not any place others were privy to. Still, what else could I do except keep going?

"But why Carolyn Gelman next?" I asked. "And why me? The phase one/two trials we're setting up won't have control groups, just patients who will get the new drugs. And hopefully benefit."

Her eyes flashed with rising anger. "I know that. But the next step will be the big phase three trials, which *will* have controls. Patients will enroll because they want the new treatments, but half of them will be denied. Even though it's already obvious that my double-antibody ADC is much better than anything else."

"If that holds up, the phase three trial would be stopped early so everyone could benefit from your drug," I pointed out. "But regardless, neither Gelman nor I would be directors of that kind of trial."

"You think I'm stupid?!" she exploded. "That you can just argue your way out of this?"

"No, I know you're not—"

Her face contorted with rage. "Shut up! I don't need you to grovel. I may have made a mistake with Gelman. But you're the director of the entire institute. Everything that goes on here is your responsibility." She raised the knife above my chest. "And now it's time for you to pay the price."

I knew it was over. She was too far gone for me to reach. My last thought before panic overwhelmed me was that I'd arranged my own death. *So stupid!*

I struggled to move before the knife came down, but it was no use. I was firmly secured, and my efforts only served to elicit a harsh laugh from her.

But suddenly, the door flung open, and I heard Karen's voice. "Drop the knife! Now!"

Shirley turned toward the door, and I could see her start to tremble when she spotted the gun in Karen's hand.

"Now!" Karen yelled again.

At that, Shirley screamed like a cornered animal and started to plunge the knife down.

But a shot rang out, and she fell to the ground.

CHAPTER 49

Karen ran over and kicked the knife away as two detectives rushed into the office. She immediately told them we were fine and gestured toward Ginger. While they examined her, Karen grabbed the knife, cut me loose, and we melted into each other's arms.

When we came up for air, one of the detectives reported that Ginger had been hit in the shoulder and would be okay.

"Good, I didn't want to kill her," Karen said.

The detective nodded. "I figured that. An ambulance is on its way. Actually two. We found some guy passed out in the lobby, maybe drugged, and he needs attention too."

I snapped back to reality. "Martin. She said she knocked him out with some kind of anesthetic. We better go check on him."

Karen followed me out to the lobby, where we found Martin, seemingly asleep where I'd left him. Unconscious but alive.

Karen felt his wrist and nodded. "His pulse is strong; he'll be okay. But what the hell's going on?" Her eyes darkened. "Did the two of you have some kind of scheme going?"

The arrival of the ambulances saved me from having to answer.

One team of EMTs went into my office, and the second came over to Martin. After a brief examination, they assured us that he would be fine, but they wanted to monitor him until he came out of it.

"Do you know what he was injected with?" one of them asked. "And when?"

"I'm not sure," I had to admit. "I think it sounded sort of like propanol."

"Could it have been propofol?"

"Yes, that's it!" I checked my watch. "Probably twenty-five to thirty minutes ago."

"Okay, he should be coming out of it any time. I don't think he needs to go to the hospital, but he won't be able to drive tonight. Is there someone who can take him home?"

"He and his partner are staying at a resort in Portland," I said. "I'll give her a call."

One of the detectives had come over and interrupted. "Hang on a minute, maybe I can help." Turning to Karen, he explained. "They're ready to take the woman to the hospital, fix a broken shoulder. Jim'll go with them and set up a guard detail. But I'm going off duty now, and I live in Portland. Want me to give him a lift?"

Karen thanked him, and the EMT said that Martin was already waking up. He was far too groggy for me to tell him what had happened, so the detective promised to brief him during the trip, and they took off while Ginger was being loaded into the ambulance.

Karen looked at me pointedly when we were alone. "Are you going to tell me what the hell this was all about?"

I groaned inwardly at the thought of telling her about it. But I couldn't put it off much longer.

"We set a trap for her, and it obviously turned into a major screw-up. I'll give you the gory details in a minute. But you talk first. How did you get here in time to save my ass? I thought you were in Augusta."

Her eyes bored into me. "I guess *screw-up* is one way to describe it. *Catastrophe* would be a better one. Brad, if I hadn't shown up, she'd have killed you! And it was just luck that I got here when I did. Zelen called a little before I got to Augusta to tell me that he'd identified the killer as the daughter of a patient who died in one of Salton's trials. I recognized her name, so I called for some backup and turned around to get you and see if we could pick her up tonight."

I couldn't believe it. "You mean Zelen figured out who she was by comparing the lists of MTRI personnel and Salton's patients?"

"Uh-huh. Then he got some of the patient's DNA from a tumor biopsy the hospital had. And that turned out to be a maternal match to the killer's DNA from the crime scene. Good solid police work, which I seem to remember you disparaged as a long shot when I told you what we were going to do. Thank God you were wrong about that."

"Thank God I was," I agreed. "And I have to admit that I set all this up because I didn't think you and Zelen would be successful."

Her face ran through a spectrum of emotions, ranging from disbelief to fury, as I took her through the trap we'd set. When I finished, her reaction was succinct.

"You goddamned idiot! How could you be so fucking stupid? All you had to do was bring me in on it, and we'd have been here to nail her before you almost got yourself killed. Which I'd say you richly deserved, if I didn't love you so goddamned much!"

I'd only seen her this angry once before. At the beginning of our relationship, we'd disagreed about a case in front of her boss. She'd been furious at me for undercutting her and had refused to have anything to do with me for weeks afterward. It wasn't an experience I wanted to repeat.

"I'm sorry, Karen. But you've got to understand. The whole setup hinged on getting her to come at me when she thought I'd be vulnerable because you were away."

She glowered at me. "I know that. And I'll admit, the way you set her up was good. But you don't think I could have faked going to Augusta and been here instead? With a couple of my men?"

I sighed. This wasn't going well. "I thought of that, but it would have been too easy for her to check. She could have done any number of things: called your office, called Augusta, put a tracker on your car. And having men here who didn't belong would have looked suspicious too. That's why I got Martin to help."

"And we know from past experience that Martin can handle a gun," she conceded. "I'll give you that much. But don't you think I'm smart enough to think of that list you rattled off? And to come up with countermeasures?"

I withered under her assault. "You're right. I should have—"

"Oh shut up, Brad! Damned right you 'should have.' You 'should have' trusted Zelen and me to do our jobs, which is what brought her down in the end. And you 'should have' had enough confidence in *me* to make me part of your plan. You goddamned idiot, you almost got yourself killed because you didn't trust me!"

She'd turned red now, with her fists tightly clenched by her side. I wasn't making this any better. I started to say, "Karen, I'm so sorry—"

But her anger suddenly burned itself out. Tears filled her eyes, and she came into my arms again. "I'm just so glad you're alive," she murmured.

We held each other for a long time. Then we both got into her car and drove home holding hands. There'd be time for us to come back and pick up my car tomorrow.

EPILOGUE

I called Martin the next morning to fill him in on everything the detective hadn't known to tell him last night. Which was most of the story, including how Ginger had suckered me and how Karen had miraculously come to the rescue.

He laughed mirthlessly when I finished. "We're a real pair of bozos, you know. Both of us just automatically trusted a bright, interested student. Has Karen forgiven you yet?"

"It took a while, but yes. How about you and Carolyn?"

"Same. She was less than thrilled when a cop brought me home last night. Thought I'd been doing some pretty heavy drinking. And then she was even less happy when I told her what had really gone down." He sighed. "Anyway, I figure the least you owe me is a good dinner after all this."

Leave it to Martin to wind up thinking about food. "I can't argue with that. When are you guys coming back down here?"

"I think Carolyn wants to stay here for a few more days, now that we can finally relax. But I found what looks to be a really good place in Portland, so why don't you and Karen come up here? I'm sure we can ring up a nice fat tab for you."

———

Martin's pick, simply called Twelve, had opened to rave reviews in 2022. It was in a reconstructed red brick building on the waterfront that, in an earlier life, had been "Building Twelve" in a large factory complex.

A waiter came over with menus as soon as we were seated, and Martin took over. "We'll all order from the prix fixe menu with wine pairing, I think. Right, everyone?"

I said, "You're the boss," while Carolyn and Karen smiled at each other. We all knew Martin relished the role of head gourmand.

"Good. Now we all get the same hors d'oeuvre, a taste of gazpacho. Then there are several choices for appetizers, but let's have the lobster rolls."

That surprised me. "Lobster rolls for an appetizer?"

"Absolutely," Martin insisted. "This place is famous for them, and they aren't like regular lobster rolls. These are served on special buttery rolls that are like flaky croissants. Trust me, you don't want to miss it."

This time we all snickered, but Martin continued unfazed. "Now for the main course, I'm sure they're all good, but I think we should go with the halibut tonight. Although there's also a nice salmon dish and, of course, steak."

Carolyn spoke first. "If you say halibut, it's halibut for me." Karen and I glanced at each other and nodded. "We're not going to break rank," she said.

Martin smiled happily and handed his menu back to the waiter. He loved it when people followed his recommendations. "Excellent, we're all set until dessert then."

"I can take that now, if you'd like," the waiter offered.

Before Martin had a chance to reply, Carolyn piped up. "The ricotta cheesecake."

"Yes, ma'am. Will that be for everyone?"

Without a moment's hesitation, Martin responded, "Of course." Leaving Karen and me laughing as the waiter left.

The gazpacho was excellent, as might be expected since local tomatoes were in season. And the lobster rolls were nothing short of spectacular. We immersed ourselves in enjoying them until every smidgen had disappeared.

Only then did Carolyn turn to Karen. "Was it hard for you not to kill her? Part of you must have wanted to."

Karen nodded. "I can't deny that. Not when I saw what she was going to do to Brad. But I'd been thinking about her while I was racing to MTRI, after Zelen told me who she was, and I realized she was sick, not evil. Like a mad dog. She didn't deserve to die, and I was so close to her that a shoulder shot was easy enough."

"I'm glad," I said. "Despite everything, she was a smart and dedicated scientist. And I think she sincerely wanted to help people. She just couldn't handle her mother's death."

Martin nodded. "I obviously didn't really know her, but she was an impressive young woman. What's going to happen to her?"

Karen took a sip of wine. "She's facing murder charges in both Maine and Massachusetts, so the two sets of prosecutors will have to figure out how to handle the case. But whichever state winds up with it, I'm pretty sure the verdict will be not guilty for reason of insanity. Meaning she'll be committed to a mental hospital rather than going to prison."

"For how long?" Carolyn asked. "Is that a life sentence?"

The main course was served, and more wine was poured before Karen had a chance to answer. We paused to taste both, and Martin pronounced them superb.

Then Karen addressed Carolyn's question. "It'll certainly be for years, but she'll get proper treatment in either state. Not like the old days, when people would simply be thrown into mental institutions to be forgotten. There's not a set time; she'll be eligible for release if and when her doctors can certify that she's no longer a danger."

"I hope she makes it," I said. "I still see the Ginger I knew, even after what she almost did to me. Not to mention killing two innocent men."

Karen's face clouded. "One innocent man," she corrected. "Salton was far from it. After what he did to his students, I can't feel sorry for him."

We were quiet after that, enjoying the halibut which, as we expected after the lobster, was exquisite. Then Martin finished his wine and turned to me.

"So Brad, when are you going to offer me a job?"

I couldn't speak, partly from shock and partly because I started choking on my last bite of fish. Finally, I recovered enough to mutter incoherently, "When am I going to *what*?"

"Recruit me to MTRI," he repeated. "After spending this many days together, Carolyn and I need to be living in the same place. And I already tried to move her to New Haven with zero success."

I looked back and forth between him and Carolyn, who had now taken his hand. "You're serious, aren't you?"

"Sure am. You've got a nice place here." He winked. "Even if it does seem to get a little violent sometimes."

Karen's eyes twinkled. "That's Maine's motto. 'The way life should be.'"

Then she signaled the waiter and told him we needed a bottle of champagne.

ACKNOWLEDGMENTS

It's a pleasure to once again express my gratitude to Alexandra Zilz and Shrabastee Chakraborty for their thoughtful critiques of the manuscript. Their comments and suggestions continue to provide invaluable advice and guidance, spanning everything from grammar to plot development.

Jennifer Caven (Mainly Words Editing) did an outstanding job editing, and Evgeniia Gurcheva designed a striking cover. I'm delighted to thank them both for their efforts.

And finally, it's always a pleasure to thank Audrey Capuano for her continuing support, patience, and suggestions.

ABOUT THE AUTHOR

Geoffrey M. Cooper is an award-winning author of medical thrillers and a 2023 Maine Literary Award Finalist in Crime Fiction. His experience as a former cancer researcher, professor, and scientific administrator at Harvard Medical School and Boston University now provides extensive background for his novels. He lives in Ogunquit, Maine.

Website: https://geofcooper.com

Reviews from readers are greatly appreciated. If you enjoyed *Betrayal of Trust*, please let other readers know by leaving your comments on Amazon or Goodreads.

ALSO BY GEOFFREY M COOPER

www.ingramcontent.com/pod-product-compliance
Lightning Source LLC
Chambersburg PA
CBHW050203120726
47903CB00002B/741